Prophecy

Also by Jacqueline Lonsdale Cuerton and published by
Ginninderra Press
The Eyes Have It
The Last Shot

Jacqueline Lonsdale Cuerton

Prophecy

& other stories

Prophecy & other stories
ISBN 978 1 76041 904 2
Copyright © text Jacqueline Lonsdale Cuerton 2020

First published 2020 by
GINNINDERRA PRESS
PO Box 3461 Port Adelaide 5015
www.ginninderrapress.com.au

Contents

Cynthia

On the ground floor, a finger kept the button depressed, holding the lift waiting for its passenger to enter and activate it further. What am I doing? the woman thought. We've come this far…we're all right…it's none of my business…I'll just go home, leave well enough alone.

As that thought was about to be acted on, another thought, unbidden, came. No, it is my business. Now I've started, I'll have to finish…though he sounded so unfriendly. As if realising for the first time that the lift was there, its brightly lit interior beckoning, the decision was made with the acceptance of later consequences. The ride up was agonising, one minute seeming too fast, the next too slow.

Tim was standing at his open doorway, waiting for the lift to arrive, the sound of that voice swirling around in his head. He wanted to believe…he didn't dare believe…but what had it said? 'We haven't met.'

The lift door opened, nothing happened. Slowly, the figure emerged. Tim's heart sank. It wasn't Cynthia. That voice, so familiar; she looked so like Cynthia yet it wasn't her. He clutched the door frame, rooted to the floor.

Looking up, the woman saw Tim and slowly advanced. 'Hello,' she said, 'I'm Tamara, your daughter.'

Somehow they were inside the unit, and Tim had slumped into a chair. Tamara stood uncertainly a metre or so inside, the unit door slowly, silently, closing behind her.

'I'm sorry,' she said. 'This must be a surprise, a shock, for you. It's, umm, not exactly easy for me, either.' Tamara had noticed the drinks table and having inherited her mother's presence of mind gestured towards it. 'Do you mind…?'

Her father looked at her blankly, following her movements, accepting the glass. 'My daughter…you're my daughter?' stammered Tim. 'Where…how, is Cynthia? Your mother, where is your mother? Oh my God, all these years…what have I done…what has she done? I have a daughter. How old are you? You must be twenty-five, twenty-six. Cynthia…no, your name – what did you say?'

With a faint smile, Tamara sat in the chair opposite. 'Tamara. Mother called me Tamara. Had I been a boy it would have been Timothy. She calls me Tam, mostly.'

Looking now at his daughter, Tim realised she wasn't exactly like Cynthia. Her eyes were a sort of grey and more serious. But there was no doubting whose daughter she was with the same lovely hair, slim body, the self-assuredness. My daughter, Tim thought, just gazing at her. I should have realised, he continued to himself. Why didn't Cynthia tell me? We would have been married; we were going to anyway, eventually… All those lost years.

As if Tamara had read his thoughts, she said, 'You know, Mother was very young, younger then, I think, than girls of the same age today, and you might remember, the age of majority was twenty-one. Mother was more than a year off that.'

Tim just looked at her, taking it in, forming his own thoughts about how it would have been.

Tamara continued gently, confirming much of what Tim had conjectured. 'As you probably know, my grandparents – well, half of them: do I have another set, still? – were against the close association between you and Mother. As they've told me many times, it was nothing against you personally.'

Tim thought again of their disapproval of him.

'But they didn't think you could provide properly for their daughter. And you were both students at the time. Thank goodness we're a bit more educated about these things today,' she added, more to herself, with that light touch of humour playing about her mouth.

Although her eyes were more serious than Cynthia's, humour

changed their colour, more green, very bright, like Cynthia's, Tim noted.

'Did you, I mean, did your mother go overseas with her parents? Where is she now? Is…is she married?' Tim asked falteringly.

'Yes, I was born in England. Grandpop and Grandma stayed for three years and since then Mum and I have spent a lot of time commuting. Well, not since we decided to stop,' she said with that sort of suppressed humour. 'Mother finished her studies and worked in London, where she met Richard. They were married between my being ten and fifteen. No, I have no half siblings.'

Tim's look of alarm subsided. Gruffly, he burst out, 'And now, where is she now?'

'She's working part-time for a small firm in St Kilda. She uses her married name for business and has kept a fairly low profile. You, on the other hand,' Tamara said with that touch of humour Tim had quickly associated with her, 'have kept a pretty high profile. It hasn't been hard for Mum to follow your career.'

She didn't mention the reported work he did for underprivileged youth or, on different pages of the broadsheet press, what he'd paid at auction for a particular work of art. The unit exuded wealth, comfort, without being ostentatious. She'd heard the stories of her father's beginnings, Irish migrant poverty, arriving in Australia when he was fourteen. Her grandparents grudgingly admitted he'd been a bright, well-mannered young man, by then having won scholarships to study law. They just wanted 'one of their own' for their daughter. One of those 'one of their own', she knew, was in jail for embezzlement. While her father was principal of his law firm.

Distraught, Tim said, 'Why hasn't she contacted me? Why have we wasted so much time?'

Tamara looked pityingly at her father. The same pity she felt for her mother. And she thought, too, that they had both lost so much time. 'You always seemed so busy, Mother said, you probably wouldn't want to start again. Why should you? She felt very badly about the way she left you. She doesn't know I'm here now, but I needed to know my father for myself, not just Mother's thoughts about you.' After a pause she added, 'And I thought you should know about me.'

Still as if he were emerging from a fog, Tim said, 'And if she knows all I think about is her, that I've imagined seeing her in the most un-likely places, that her image kept coming between me and Martha, my wife, my ex-wife, will she see me?'

'Oh, Dad, Dad, I'm saying that to you now. Always referred to you as Dad – Dad's in the paper again, won this case, that case, provided funds for Aboriginal children to attend schools, colleges, universities – I like that.'

There was silence until Tim noticed his empty glass. 'Would you like another? Or a coffee, tea, something?' Looking at Tamara as if really seeing her for the first time.

'Coffee would be lovely. Thanks.' She rose with her father, following him to the kitchen, watching as he brewed the coffee, took out some cheeses, biscuits. 'Did you ever try to find Mum?'

'In the beginning, yes, I did. I dropped out of uni for a semester, then failed a year. Your grandparents did a great job in covering tracks. No one would give me any information and your mother had told me, that last day before semester started again, that she was leaving, they were all leaving, for a year in the UK. She just disappeared. Already her phone was disconnected at her flat. There was a caretaker at the big house. They could have disappeared in a puff of smoke.'

The tray was placed on a table, they resumed their chairs.

'Will she, do you think, see me?' Tim asked again. 'So much wasted time. Is she happy? Are you happy? A grown daughter I know nothing about.'

The fog was clearing but Tim was afraid that when it cleared com-pletely he would find the whole episode had been an illusion. 'How can I contact her? Will you let me see you again, let me know you? A daughter. I'm glad, glad I have a child,' he said slowly.

'Well,' replied Tamara, as if she'd known all along what she would do, 'I'll tell Mum I've seen you. I'll give you her home phone number. Take it from there.' She stopped. Looking at her father, she could see the love in his eyes, knowing it was for her as well as her mother. 'If you want to meet, I could cook dinner for you at my unit, give you a key, Mum has one, make myself scarce for the night?' Her face danced with that smile.

Tim stood and paced the floor. Stopping in front of the large window, looking out at the lines and arcs of brightness made by moving vehicles, he thought, somewhere Cynthia is out there; has been out there all this time.

Tamara joined him, slipping her arm through his.

Tim drew her to him in a hug. 'My daughter,' he said. 'I've missed so much. We've a lot to catch up on, haven't we?'

'Yes,' she said softly.

'What if Cynthia doesn't like me any more?' Tim wondered.

'Not much chance of that. What if you don't like her?' Tamara teased. 'Mother might have middle-age spread, grey hair and wear glasses.'

'Does she?'

'She uses reading glasses.' Tamara looked enquiringly at her father. 'Are you amenable to my plan?'

'Makes sense,' replied Tim. 'Not exactly neutral space but at least not your mother's place and not mine. Quiet and private.' But with some concern for his daughter, he continued, 'What about you? What will you do for the evening?'

Giving Tim a squeeze she said, 'Oh, don't worry about me. I could work – I'm a pathologist at the hospital – or spend the weekend at Grandpop's and Grandma's, let them know what's happening. Are your parents still alive, around? I could go and meet them,' she added mischievously, 'but I wouldn't want to alarm them, give them heart attacks or anything, or I could agree to my boyfriend's suggestion that we go off for the weekend.'

'Yes, of course. Enough of the office chatter gets through my skull so I know some of what young people get to these days,' Tim smiled.

'And my parents? Yes, they're still around. Not in Heidelberg, though, the suburb your grandfather didn't think much of. They've "moved up" in the world, your grandfather would be pleased to know.'

'They must have hurt you terribly.'

'I suppose, in a way, his attitude gave me the extra impetus to do well. My own parents didn't push, but when I think of the sacrifices they made, to provide me with an education – not free and no HECCS in those days…so, I'm not unhappy with what I've achieved,' Tim mused.

The following few weeks were a nightmare for Tim. He needed to talk to his parents first, let them know what had happened. He visited them for their soft, calming demeanour. He and Cynthia spoke several times on the phone, tears were shed by both. He met with Tamara for several lunchtime coffees and twice her boyfriend accompanied her. A night was settled on for the dinner.

He pressed the buzzer in case Cynthia had arrived already but with no reply, Tim let himself into the building and up to his daughter's unit. The table was beautifully set and looking around Tim took in the quiet elegance. There were a couple of paintings and ornaments he recognised from the Reynolds' house so long ago, part of the wealth, the supposed background that Cynthia's parents believed should separate them. One wall was lined with books and, in a corner, a half-size harp. Cynthia has taught her well, he thought.

Lost in the discovery of his daughter, he was calmer now. Walking over to the books, he ran his hand along them, not really taking in the titles. He stopped, lost in his thoughts.

For the last few moments he had been observed. Since Tamara's intervention, Cynthia had been in a turmoil. The feelings of the past quarter century had become hopelessly tangled: her love for the young Tim, the intense pain and anger when she had to leave him, the fierce love she had for her daughter, the baby her parents had forbidden her to tell Tim about, the pride she'd felt at Tim's successes, sorrow for the two people they'd briefly married. And now, were they the same people? Could they communicate as they had so long ago; could they love each other?

Sensing he wasn't alone, Tim slowly turned. For what seemed like an eternity, they just looked, each drinking in every detail of the other. Slowly, painfully, they moved towards each other. Lost in each other's arms, the lost time, the pain, the uncertainty faded to nothing.

Later there was soft music, the talk flowed freely and occasionally the tinkle of Cynthia's laughter skipped in the spaces of the room.

Heaven Sent

'Have another piece of angel cake. It's lovely, isn't it, one of my favourites.' Marie, elegantly clad, mid-sixties, was holding the plate towards her son, Henri. 'When's this baby of yours due?'

'Middle of next month. You know that. Why?' He took a piece of the light-as-air cake.

'Oh, I don't know…thinking of your grandmother – perhaps she's thinking of coming back. She always said she would. I feel as if she's been, umm, sort of here, flitting about. Thinking about her more than usual. But do you know, I simply could not make this cake when she was alive and now it really does seem to be weightless. Are angels weightless?'

'Keep on like this, Mum, and you'll be a candidate for the psychiatric ward. And when Grandma said she was coming back, was it to haunt you or just be here?'

'Oh, you know how your grandmother was – always interested in everything. You discussed the state of the world with her often enough. Wouldn't we all like to know how things turn out in fifty, a hundred years?'

'Yes, but she's been dead for only five. And as far as I'm concerned, she's going to stay dead. Oh, my stars,' Henri suddenly realised where his mother's thoughts were leading, 'you're not thinking she might be reborn as my child, are you?'

'Well, many people do believe in reincarnation.'

'And what I know of it, I don't think they have a choice about what or who they come back as. Hindus, Buddhists and I don't know who else, say it depends on the kind of life, or lives, you've already lived. You've been talking to my friend Raj too much.'

'No,' his mother said slowly, 'For some reason I remembered my grandfather. He was always very nice, kind, but he and I were not that close. Your Aunt Elise was his favourite. But when you and your cousins were toddlers and Elise and I lived on opposite sides of the world, I heard my grandfather's voice, as clear as yours is now. And he'd been dead for several years. And don't tell me I dreamt it,' she said to Henri's attempted interruption.

'So, tell me then, what did he say?'

'Well, it was a message about Elise. He was telling me she was in some kind of trouble. In those days, we used to write letters. I'd had one from her about three weeks prior to this event and she seemed to be happy enough. Usual things with two small boys. Anyway, I felt strongly enough about it to get up and telephone. She admitted she had sealed the windows and doors of their flat and was about to turn on the gas. Didn't go into the whys and wherefores then, but we did talk. As soon as we hung up, I found the phone number of her local police station and asked them to go round. Anyway, I believe that had I not heard the voice of my grandfather, she and the two boys wouldn't be alive today. So one has to think about the energy part of us and what happens to it when the body fails.'

'I simply cannot imagine having my grandmother as my child. Wonder what Amalie would think about it. She and the old lady did get along. I think of all the girlfriends I'd had, Amalie was her favourite. I'm glad she made it to our wedding. But now the old girl is dead and going to stay that way, thank you very much. The only connection she will have with our child is through inherited genes.'

'I didn't ever ask you, but after being so firm about your not ever having children, how come…well, what changed your mind?'

'None of your business, really, Mother dear.' Henri grinned.

*

'And indeed it isn't.' Josephine tossed her head and broke off another piece of cloud that in her domain tasted like pavlova. 'Come on, Helene, want to play golf?'

And for no apparent reason the crystal beads that hung around the base of a lampshade in Henri's mother's house moved enough to make a noise as they gently clashed together.

The golfing gear suddenly appeared and the two friends started their round of a course that could have been – well, it was, wasn't it? – made in heaven. High-ranking golfers on earth might say they'd die for it if they knew about it.

'That daughter of mine thinks too much,' said Josie, hitting her ball rather too strongly and landing it in the rough.

'Well, she's your daughter, what do you expect?' asked Helene. 'And do be careful, Josie. You know you cause some mishap or other every time you…well, you know, lose your temper, even slightly.'

'That last flood had nothing to do with me. And anyway, they need to have a little shake now and then. It's the only way to make the silly people think. If they took notice of the hints we send down, they wouldn't be in the mess they are now. Anyway, I lose a ball, you win, and you know children love hailstones,' Jossie replied with a toss of her head, at the same time flicking the gold club away from her.

'Now you've added lightning. Honestly, Josie, why do you do it?'

'Why not?' returned Josie. 'Hail isn't altogether bad. Like I said, kids love it and with their body heat it soon melts. If it's bigger pieces and damages stuff, plumbers do well, people get new cars, carpets, roofs, all manner of things. Keeps people in business. And a little lightning or thunder spices up the ghost stories. Don't be so stuffy, Helene.'

'You're totally wicked, Josie. I don't know how you managed to land up here in the first place; you could get away with…'

'Oh, no, not that. I'd never get away with it and I've never considered it. Well,' amended Josie quickly as a green cloud approached, 'I might have considered it but with no real intention, as you know.' she finished and the green cloud disappeared. 'And this is Heaven, need I remind you, and we're supposed to enjoy ourselves. Many more goody-two-shoes like you, Helene, and I'd think I was in the Other Place. Oh, I'm sorry, sorry, don't cry like that, Helene – you'll create a flood somewhere. Here, have some meringue. Imagine flavours in the pink range, strawberry, watermelon, cherry, might stretch to peach,' Josie consoled as she broke off a piece of fluffy cloud, pale gold underneath with red-pinks mingled through the top.

Helene was happily munching, but very tidily, not dropping a single crumb. 'Have you, er, ever thought of, you know…?'

'What, Helene? Whatever are you trying to say?'

'Please don't be cross with me, Josie. It's just that we're such good friends and I'd feel, well, lonely, if you, you know, decided to go back.'

'Well, it's not exactly my decision, is it? It's up to the Elders. As you know. Didn't you ever want to go back, try to improve things?'

Helene shook. 'Oh, no. I could never make up my mind about anything. All I did was make people cross and probably behave in ways they otherwise might not if I hadn't been around.'

'Well, it's no good thinking about it,' Josie said. 'It's out of my hands.'

Josie had, however, made an appointment to see the Panel on the day of her arrival. She'd never had any intention of staying in Heaven after she'd arranged things to her satisfaction. Henri, her handsome grandson, and his lovely wife were the ideal pair. His first partner hadn't been quite right, lovely girl but not for him, and while it had caused more pain for him than for her, he was happy now. Josie made sure the rejected girl soon found her right partner and they were now a happy couple with two children. It had taken a little longer to engineer Amalie and Henri into the same place at the same time but the impact had been so spectacular they'd almost set the place on fire. So right for each other – alike in many ways, very different in others. The other two grandsons were doing well and being looked after but she had a special soft spot for Henri.

Now, you should know that Heaven is a multicultural, multiracial place of people with good intent. In Earth life, they might not have agreed with one another, but up here, they all instantly saw the other's point of view. Members of the Panel were many but each time it convened, it was usually only a part of the whole. The choice was dependent upon the matter under discussion.

Josie had been before the Panel several times and this one was taking place some little time after the last conversation with Helene. It included Saints Peter, Francis, Augustine, Cecelia; the founder of Buddhism, Siddhartha Gautama; and Krishna, representing the Hindus. Confucius and Yahweh were there as well. Josie had already spoken with Avatars like Ganesha, the elephant god and remover of obstacles, and Lakshmi, goddess of wealth and education. Mencius, known as the Second Sage of the Confucian heritage, and who believed in the goodness of human nature and was totally opposed to tyrannical authority, floated about nearby along with several interested others. This child about to be born on Earth was going to be well-equipped to do great things. And it wouldn't be so unusual, as both parents were well-endowed with brainpower.

'Well,' intoned Ganesha, 'you have applied to return to Earth almost immediately. It has also come to our attention that you have been quietly seeking counsel from various souls whose qualities you wish to acquire.'

'At the same time,' interposed Saint Francis, 'you have made quite a name for yourself among the population. If such things as indigestion or headache existed here, many would be seeking medications on account of your behaviour. As it is, you have ruffled many feathers. Do you think you have the necessary qualities for a return?'

Ever inscrutable, Confucius asked if Josephine was aware of the great responsibility she was wishing to assume. 'Tyranny,' he said, 'seems to have become the god on Earth. In the name of just about all of us, unfortunately.' he added quietly. 'What do you have to say for yourself?'

'We-ell,' replied Josie slowly, for she knew she had to answer carefully, any ill-conceived ideas would be pounced upon immediately. 'I know it's not usual to apply to return to a particular body, that being the decision of more learned souls such as yourselves. I also know I wasn't a perfect person and, as you point out, the state of the world is chaotic, which is why my grandson didn't want to add to it. He isn't able to see a happy future for anyone being born in these times. However, we know differently and the world needs people with the combined qualities of those such as my grandson and his partner, with a few more that I believe I can provide. I may have ruffled feathers but, if I may say so, every soul likes me and welcomes me with a smile…'

The panel hid its collective smile at this.

'…and I believe, if allowed to go as my grandson and his wife's child, they will gain in strength and do more than they do already, which is considerable. And while I have no control over others' actions once I am there, I believe, if granted the qualities I seek, I, I mean the child, can rise to a position of influence.'

'You are not thinking of taking pride with you as well, I hope,' said Siddhartha severely.

'No, no, but there's nothing wrong with healthy and humble ambition,' Josie replied quickly.

'Have you thought that in being humble and quiet you might exert more influence than someone who has position and money, in many cases alienating in themselves? It seems to me, Angel Josephine, it would be a task to reduce the ruthless ambition that still is within.'

Josie opened her mouth to protest but Saint Frances looked hard at her, warning her to remain quiet.

'While we consider your case,' tinkled the musical and bell-like tones of Saint Cecelia, 'go and have a nice, quiet game of tennis with Helene, whom you ruffle more than any other and who would miss you the most if you go. Off you go.'

'Just a moment, Josephine. You realise of course, that if you do leave here, your memory is wiped clean of all that went before,' enquired Saint Augustine, 'even while it is impossible to give anyone a complete make-over and remove totally all of the most extreme habits you had in your life?' while Krishna and Cecelia harmonised on flute and harp.

'Yes,' she said, looking at them all, 'but with your good grace I would have a Guardian Angel and the qualities I desire, would, I know, make a difference.' And Josie floated off to be with Helene.

Of course the decision had been made before the interview began, some things never change, but it didn't hurt to remind the souls what a little anxiety felt like. What the Panel needed to work out was the actual mix that would make up Josie's new personality. Not entirely new, of course – as St Augustine said, a little bit of us keeps going.

*

Amalie, looking radiant, put her hand on Henri's arm. 'Darling,' she said, 'I think you'd better ring my parents and your mum, and take me to the birthing centre.'

A few hours later, grandparents, proud parents and sleeping son were in a bright, flower-filled room. Amalie was tired but looked beautiful. Henri seemed to have a grin firmly attached to his face and the good-natured sleeping child seemed impervious to his being passed back and forth between his parents. The three grandparents looked on fondly. If one looked closely, Marie could be accused of a slight smugness, but the attention was not on her.

'What are you going to call him?' she asked.

'Don't know,' replied Henri. 'How about Simon?'

'Or Kris,' said Amalie.

'What about Auguste?' from Henri.

'Or Cecil, for you, Pops.'

'Or Sidney or Francis.'

'Or Joseph,' murmured Josie's daughter.

And Joseph the boy became. He is still a child, passing all the accepted milestones. He whinged when he was teething and cried when he was cold or hungry but there are never any arguments, no selfish acts of not sharing within his group of friends and companions. He is popular at school where his teachers love him and the students in the classes Joseph attends have all raised their academic levels by several points.

We shall have to wait and see, won't we?

Hot Gravy

It was really the sight of him crawling around on the floor, trying to clean up the mess while gravy still slid off his normally shiny bright straight hair, that decided her. He'd got back late, very late, from playing the piano at the restaurant. She'd quietly asked if he was still hungry and was he sure he wasn't too tired to eat while she noted the red angora fluff stuck to the front, shoulders, arms of his light grey suit. The kind that comes off female sweaters when there's friction with another body.

He'd seemed taken aback by her considerate tone and acceptance of his working late excuse. Certainly, he'd brought flowers, from the restaurant's desk and why throw them out? But he'd thought she might be just a little cross. If it pleased her to eat the dinner she'd saved for him, he would, and he sat at the table at her bidding. The aroma from the opened oven door was indeed a pleasure, and his salivary glands went to work at the anticipated delicious meal to come. She approached, with steaming plate, as he spread his napkin across his lap. His surprise, therefore, was great when the dinner ended not on the table but tipped over his head.

He jumped up, upsetting his chair and shaking his head, yelling, 'What…?'

She thought the red fluff, now wet with gravy, looked like old blood. 'You lying bastard,' Janelle spat, 'you've been with her. I know you've been carrying on. Get up and get out, you stupid, inconsequential little man.'

By this time, he was on all fours, trying, without success, to clean up the mess. 'Oh, please Janelle,' he begged, 'you know it means nothing. You know how she is, you know I love you. Please let me stay. It's late and it's raining. I'll sleep on the settee. I'll clean this up and sleep on the settee. In the morning we'll talk.'

'No, we won't. You won't.' she said. 'Get out. Go and have a hot bath at her house – her husband might lend you a pair of pyjamas.'

He'd stood by this time and looked pathetic but he seemed to know he'd lost and meekly opened the door and left.

Janelle was angry, but more at herself for being taken in than at his behaviour. Nevertheless, she collected what few belongings he'd left at her apartment and threw them out of the window onto the wet grass one floor down. Next morning, she saw one lone sock, which was eventually shredded by the lawnmower.

It had never been anything deep and meaningful. True, he played the piano beautifully and sometimes she went to the restaurant and someone would dance with her. It was on one of these occasions that she met the woman in red angora. It seemed to be her favourite dress. She'd even had the impertinence to take him away from the piano to dance with her. The violinist played something floaty but she was too heavy to do it justice. Janelle had never taken him from the piano; he was there to play, it was his job. But he was weak.

He had his own flat but the nights they spent together were always at Janelle's house; she'd never been to his place. Weekends, days off, they'd go for picnics in his sports car. He was devastatingly good-looking, a bit of a trophy to show off. He said he was Hungarian but never talked about it or any family. On occasion, Janelle had stray thoughts about his legal status, but they were fleeting. There'd been a certain emptiness in the relationship; they didn't see films together, he appeared not to read, they didn't discuss politics or religion. But he did make love, beautifully. The night of the upturned dinner had been waiting to happen, or something like it – an excuse to break the affair.

Janelle heard no more from him or of him. It was almost as if he never existed. One evening, when she'd just got in from work, there was a knock at the door. Thinking it was a same-floor neighbour, who often required a cup of sugar, or flour, or just a bit of tea, otherwise there would have been a buzz on the intercom, Janelle opened it to two policemen. Taken aback, she demanded to know how they got into the building and to see their ID. They identified themselves, saying they had come in when someone else was leaving and everyone trusts a cop, no? They then ascertained that Janelle was who they wanted to talk to and suggested they come inside. Janelle's first thought was the health and safety of her family: had something happened to one or more of them?

'No, as far as we know, your family is safe and well,' replied the detective sergeant, as he took a seat on the settee and the young constable more deferentially sat on the edge of a chair.

The constable took a photograph from a folder. 'We're making enquiries about this man,' he said. 'We understand he's a friend of yours.'

'Yes,' replied Janelle, 'I know, knew him. We're no longer friends. I haven't seen or heard from him for several weeks. What has happened to him?'

'How did you meet him?'

'At the restaurant, that one, where he plays the piano,' she said, pointing to the photo. 'Or should I say played, as you seem to be looking for him.'

'When? When did you meet him, Miss er, Hassle?'

'Hazzle. Zeds, it's spelled with zeds. About nine months ago and I haven't had anything to do with him for about three months.'

'And why did the association end, Miss Hazzle?'

'For the same reason any association ends, I suppose,' Janelle replied tartly. 'It had become meaningless. And while you're asking me all these questions, I should ask you one – why do you want to know? Why should I tell you anything at all?'

'We're just putting together a profile, Miss Hazzle,' replied the detective sergeant, who, Janelle had noticed, had been taking a good look around the lounge room from where he sat.

'Didn't think he was that interesting,' muttered Janelle almost under her breath.

The young constable took a quick look at the senior officer.

The detective, good-looking, Janelle had noted, asked, 'And what was the meaning in the beginning, if you don't mind, Miss Hazzle?'

She looked at him, thinking hmm. 'When I think about it,' she said, 'I don't really know. I heard him playing the piano at the restaurant, like I said, and a love of music seems to have been the only connection.' The fact that he was a great lover she thought she could keep to herself.

'Have you ever been to his place of living, Miss Hazzle?'

'Well, no, I haven't,' replied Janelle. 'I don't think I even know the address, except it's on the north side. He has a mobile phone and work, I didn't need to know where he lived. Uh oh, perhaps he has a wife and five children,' she laughed.

'Perhaps he has,' said the officer.

There were more questions, about any travel she had undertaken, the destinations and duration of her stay. Any people she knew in those locations and who she spent her time with now. She could have become defensive about this questioning but Janelle had a government position, a good security rating and the police could have found any of this information on her file. Probably had, so why make a fuss.

'Thank you for your time, Miss Hazzle.' The detective sergeant stood up. 'If you think of anything we might like to hear about, any new information, please ring me,' and he handed her his card.

The constable hastily got to his feet and rushed to open the door.

Following, to see them out, Janelle said she couldn't imagine there'd be anything else they needed to know from her and whatever it was they thought he'd done would soon be sorted. 'Couldn't be too bad,' she remarked. 'I mean, he's so mild, inoffensive. Wouldn't say boo to a goose.'

Janelle made herself a fresh coffee and sat on her settee, just about where the nice-looking detective sergeant had been. Why on earth would they be interested in Miki, she thought. Domestic violence? No. Wife or child maintenance? A possibility. Tax evasion? Could be, but the questioning really didn't indicate anything like those things. Oh, well, her mind continued, who cares? Maybe red angora's husband is suing for something. Good luck to him.

The young constable asked his senior what he thought. 'Do you think she knows anything, sarge?'

'No,' came the curt reply.

Life went on in its usual way. Janelle went to work every day, saw the occasional film with a girl friend, and sometimes two or three of them would go out for a meal. She missed the picnics and the sports car and listened to music on her own.

Then about three months after the visit of the policemen, she arrived at work to find several of her colleagues gathered together at the reception desk, talking animatedly over a newspaper.

'Hey, what's going on?' she wanted to know.

'You mean you haven't heard? It was on the news last night,' one of them said. 'Here, have a look,' and the group separated to let her in.

She saw a picture of Miki between two large men who were obviously not allowing him the freedom to go anywhere but where they dictated.

Janelle looked around at the gathering and scooping up the newspaper said, 'Do you mind?' and took it to her office to read alone and in more comfort. She learned that Miki had a list of aliases and had been under surveillance for some time. That means I have, too, she thought, continuing to read.

Apparently he was in the pay of a middle eastern country to which he had been selling secrets. Oh, my goodness, thought Janelle, her hand flying to her mouth, they'll be arresting me next. She quickly grabbed her bag, frantically searching for the card of the police officer, all the while continuing to read. She noticed a smaller photo, which required a closer look, and she recognised the image of red angora behind a man said to be her husband. Well, well, well, her thoughts swirled, how interesting. By this time, her fingers had located the card and with slight shaking, dialled the number.

'Hello, could I speak to Detective Sergeant Pollinger, please?'

'Speaking.'

'Yes, it's Janelle Hazzle here,' at which point she seemed to have run out of words.

'What can I do for you, Miss Hazzle?'

'Sergeant, Detective, sorry, Pollinger, I've just read the paper – about Miki Stavosch. I…I had no idea…' and she trailed off again. 'I mean… I didn't know. You have to believe me. I wouldn't…'

A slight smile was playing around the mouth of Detective Sergeant Pollinger, while his fingers played with the coils of the telephone cord. 'As you haven't heard from us again and you haven't been arrested, I think we can take it that you are in the clear, Miss Hazzle,' came the laconic response. 'However, I would like to talk to you again, on another matter…'

Janelle paled.

'…perhaps this evening? I think it would be better if we used some neutral place, not Miki's restaurant, it's been closed down, ha, ha. Shall I pick you up at seven and we'll take it from there?'

After some jumbled words of acquiescence, Janelle put the phone down only to pick it up again to ring through to her boss. A little later she was seated in one of the easy chairs in his office and gratefully drinking the coffee the secretary had brought her. 'You must have known about this, Stan,' she said, slightly accusingly, pointing to the paper on his desk.

'Afraid so,' Stan said, 'but I couldn't tell you anything, You understand that. And of course we've had a watch on you, more for your safety than anything else. I know my staff, Janelle, and you were never under any suspicion. It just had to be kept to a need to know basis.'

'So why does Detective Sergeant Pollinger need to speak to me again?' she asked, colouring slightly.

Stan looked over his glasses at her. 'And where is this, er, interview, taking place?'

Tracing a pattern in the carpet, Janelle repeated what the detective had said to which Stan replied that he didn't think Janelle had too much to worry about.

Promptly at seven, the intercom buzzed and Janelle asked Detective Sergeant Pollinger if he would like to come up or should she go down.

'Down,' he said and soon they were in his car and out on the highway.

'Where are you taking me?' asked a slightly nervous Janelle.

'You'll see,' was all she got in reply.

On a headland a little way up the coast, she saw a building looking something like the Greek Parthenon. 'Oh,' she breathed, 'I've always wanted to come here. How? You must have done some rigorous homework on me,' she finished ruefully.

'Well, some, of course, but I saw the book on Greek history on your coffee table. With a bookmark in it. It's one of my interests, too. Have you been? No, of course you haven't. Come on, let's see if the food matches the architecture and you can tell me something I don't know.'

He opened the car door and helped her out, holding her hand slightly longer than was absolutely necessary. But Janelle was in no rush to retrieve it, either.

It's Not Cricket

It just wasn't cricket. There they were, my two parents, not long before Christmas, watching an international one-day match. Can't see the sense of it, myself. My grandmother and I agreed on many things, and the idiocy of sport in general, and cricket in particular, was one of them, but golf was a very close second. If you want to take a walk, just walk, with a friend or two. Look at the flowers and trees. Get down on your haunches to look at moss or tiny plants instead of bending in the middle to fish a hard, small, white ball, out of a hole only to hit it again with a metal stick. You want upper body exercise? Swing from a tree, with your child; you stretch the whole body then, instead of just half. But like I said, my parents were at a one-dayer, bad enough, but can you imagine sitting there for five! Insane, if you ask me.

Well, there they were, my mum and dad, on hard seats in the stand. A couple of seats along sat a couple of young Indian fellows. I understand cricket has long been one of their favourite sports. Must have been introduced by the British. I suppose there were some positives to Britain's various colonisations – this story wouldn't have happened if the previous history hadn't, and of course, the Brits took their sport with them.

My mum, being my mum, asked the fellows if they were enjoying the game and what part of India they were from. Subtle, my Mum, letting them know she knew where they were from nationally, and giving them an opportunity to open up. Their families were from Gujarat, they said, but now they lived in Fiji. Born there themselves, so they were Fiji Indians. Now I knew that it was from Gujarat that the British – them again, but before you say anything I have to tell you I am one myself – anyway, the Brits took Indians to Fiji as indentured labour. The Brits had found the Fijians weren't really amenable to working in the fields cutting sugar cane for somebody else. So while the British still had some influence, they persuaded the Indians to go. Many stayed behind at the end of their terms and some small migration from India followed.

My mum was a very chatty person and, thinking these two fellows looked like high school students, asked why they were taking a day off school. They laughed at that and said they were university students and on vacation. Mum shifted gear then and started talking about politics, the British in India and Fiji, the economy, education, art and literature. You can cover a lot of subjects in a day at the cricket. I mean, those chaps who are standing about waiting for something to happen could write a thesis in that time. But I don't think sportspeople are all that bright. On the other hand, maybe they are because there can be a lot of money in it. And after all, if that's what they're good at and it amuses others, where's the harm? Same could be said of play-acting and there isn't the same amount of money in that.

I never have found out what maidens in slips are, or silly mid-ons. But, as I was saying, Christmas was approaching and my mum, ever ready for a party, invited them home for the day, saying they would no doubt not be having any celebration themselves. They thanked her but said they shared a house with three others and they'd be spending the day together with some of the off-duty student nurses and students of other things. Mum said something about it being a shame, perhaps they would like to come in the week before New Year. She can be insistent, my mum, and a day was settled on: the five house-sharers would come for lunch midway through the week. The two young chaps insisted on bringing some of their dishes along, not the usual habit of Indians – or the English, either. Perhaps they thought our food would be all meat and there'd be nothing they could eat.

Poor Dad hardly ever got a word in but he might have blanched at that, thinking he was going to have a restful week. Dad learned long ago that if he wanted a peaceful life, he needed to fall in with Mum's plans. Mind you, when he stood firm on any issue, he was rock-solid. There'd be a few fireworks or mild-to-medium hysterics but Dad would just say that was his position and that was that. No shifting him at all. When I was growing up, I used to think, oh, easy-peasy, and it was true, I could get so far, but I'd forget, every time, when I'd try to take that extra liberty, there was an indestructible brick wall.

The chaps might have been surprised at such an invitation from a Westerner but I learned later, Indians are spur-of-the-moment people and are just as likely to invite a group of foreigners to their homes as we are to invite a friend in for a cup of tea.

I should tell you here, my mum's background was very mixed. Her dad had grown up in Burma and there's a bit of Burmese blood in there somewhere. My mum was born in England but connections with the East continued. Grandpa had some brothers and sisters still there, with their growing families. As it happened, there were connections with practically everywhere else as well, which added greatly to my own education.

In the evening, I was told of the invitation and that I had better keep that day free. I just rolled my eyes and said something about one of these days her impromptu invitations would end up with our being beaten, robbed or worse. Conversation then revolved around the five young men and how good they were – leaving home and family, things familiar, having to learn how to housekeep, cook. You remember, in those days not many men did anything around the house in a domestic fashion. Goodness, I can recall older friends about to give birth, cooking endless meals to put in freezers so that the poor husbands, soon-to-be fathers, wouldn't starve. My own culinary skills were next to nil so these paragons of virtue were being held up in front of me.

'You'd do well, my girl,' my mum had said, 'to put more time into your studies, make a proper commitment to something instead of all the time you spend at that play-acting. And you could help me in the kitchen a bit more.'

Looking back, I can only suppose that meeting up with these young Indians had reawakened some long-buried values in her. I mean, I had a fairly easy time of it, everything was at my doorstep; I didn't have to give up anything, go to a foreign culture, in order to further educate myself. I was living an almost hedonistic lifestyle.

But she was no philistine, my mum. She'd grown up in England and family friends included some of the literary greats of the time such as George Bernard Shaw and Evelyn Waugh. She enjoyed theatre, books and music. She hadn't minded when I joined the amateur dramatics society and often came to performances. In between, I was dabbling about with a BA at university and my sentiment was, a pass is a pass is a pass. And it was she who frequently shooed me out of the kitchen.

With the advent of the Foreign Five, it seemed suddenly I wasn't doing enough. I got the impression I was expected to bring glory, if not to my country then at least to my family. They were being noble, I wasn't. Cricket, I thought, has a lot to answer for. However, I did point out to her that she should think about how many overseas professional theatre performances she saw in a year and how much work was being done with traumatised children through drama. That quietened her a bit but I was getting sick of having to defend myself and thought it about time I met these models of perfection.

Like I said, my grandfather had been born in Burma and he had travelled a fair bit with my grandmother, my mum and Aunt Daphne, so our tastes in food were many and varied. My skills came in useful when it came to decorating the house and, if I do say so myself, on that occasion it looked pretty good by the time I'd finished. I'd done a bit of research and found the Hindu script for the words 'peace', 'health', and 'long life', drawn them on coloured card, cut out and strung them across various doorways. Pleased my mum no end.

I drew the line, though, at wearing the sari she'd pulled out from somewhere. At every opportunity, she'd been telling me I had to behave with decorum. She said I could do worse than set my cap at any one of them and do well, as they all had such good prospects. I think my mum must have got that straight out of *Pride and Prejudice*. My mum is not without her flights of fancy. And anyway, I wasn't exactly friendless, just not looking for a mate. Marriage, babies and helpless males just didn't appeal. She said if I wouldn't wear the sari then I should wear something decent and not show too much flesh. Furthermore, I was not to tell any jokes, especially my more obscure ones, as they have a different sense of humour.

Dad said I was too young to be thinking of marriage and why marry a foreigner when it would probably mean I'd have to go to his country to live. As I said, my dad does occasionally speak up so I piled it on about how one reads of the ill-treatment of Indian daughters-in-law, forgetting to mention it was almost always in rural villages and the incidence is probably as often, or seldom, as someone being murdered here. I continued that the older generation probably didn't speak English, and, in any case, it was likely all the boys were already engaged, betrothals sometimes taking place cot to cot.

Anyway, I was having too much fun with my uni friends and the theatre crowd. I told my mum she was being a selfish cow because she was using me to reintroduce her to a once familiar way of life. Then, of course, I got a long lecture on India's sacred cows and would I please mind my language. Dad told me not to be rude. I was beginning to wish I'd taken a trip to China for the season – anywhere but here.

The day arrived. The weather was truly tropically hot and sticky. Tempers were stretched to breaking and I could not fathom why my mum set so much store by my getting on with our visitors. Or at least one of them. Even poor old Dad was getting stroppy and snapped at me. Of course he apologised, saying it was the weather and my mum carrying on so.

I had devised an exit plan whereby one of my theatre friends was to ring at two-thirty and say it was essential that I go to the rehearsal hall immediately as there'd been a fire and some costumes had, apparently, been damaged. We had a New Year's Eve production and needed to sort things out. I thought I could manage through the business of lunch and even had a giggle wondering how these very proper fellows would cope with the silly Christmas hats – my mum had insisted on putting out the leftover bonbons.

Aunt Daphne and my cousins Phoebe, by then fifteen, and Clarissa, nearly fourteen, always spent Christmas with us, so they were invited to the lunch too. My grandma was on a Christmas cruise. Aunt Daph was actually divorced but in those days we didn't talk about it. She and Mum had cooked another turkey and all the trimmings, lots of veg cooked separately from any meat juices but which would, no doubt, be delicious. To follow, we had another plum pudding and brandy sauce. Dad always insisted on pouring brandy over the pudding and setting fire to it when it came to the table. Looked great and tasted wonderful.

We always complained about the heat and why did we insist on this traditional feast but my mum just wouldn't hear of doing it differently and here we were, doing it again. It's a wonder we didn't ever suffer heart attacks over the jolly season. Aunt Daphne was looking forward to meeting the Foreign Five and she liked cricket, too, so they had something to talk about. Phoebe and Clarissa were ridiculously excited; their lives were overprotected, I thought. They attended a girls' school, poor Aunt Daph probably trying to keep them away from the 'wicked ways of the opposite sex' for as long as possible.

At noon sharp, a car pulled up and four suit and tie fellows climbed out. My mum whispered that she thought they could have relaxed a bit for today. Dad was in shorts and bright shirt, Mum a nice skirt and blouse, Aunt and cousins had on comfortable cotton dresses and I was wearing a sort of 30s-style dress with a low waist, wide sash, mid-calf length and sleeveless in a nice, cool white. Next to suited four, though, we looked like street urchins.

Ah, but wait! Here is mystery man, number five, busying himself at the car boot, taking out baskets from which aromas of the contents were beginning to reach us. He asked the other fellows to give him a hand and two took a basket each and number five turned and took out one more. I could see it contained flowers. He brought up the rear but already I could see he was drop-dead gorgeous. (That expression hadn't been invented then so I probably would have thought he was scrumptious or something.) He had a beaming smile and looked comfortable in slacks, short-sleeve shirt and sandals.

I was introduced to the foreign two, then they were introduced to Aunt Daphne, Phoebe and Clarissa, and then the other three were introduced to us. Still on the veranda, which was the coolest part of our house, Number Five presented Mum with a lovely bouquet of flowers, Dad a bottle of Scotch and me a smaller bunch of flowers. He sort of bowed to Aunt Daphne and the too-pink, slightly awkward girls, apologising for the lack of more flowers but he hadn't known, et cetera. However, still standing next to me, he reached out and took three blooms from my bunch, saying he was sure this lovely lady wouldn't mind, and gave one each to the three. They all beamed like bright gerberas in the sun.

My mum suggested we go and put the flowers in water and Dad said we should all sit down and could he get the fellows a beer, perhaps. Number Five said he'd love one but the other four didn't drink so Dad asked Phoebe to get soft drinks for them. Dad took two bottles from the esky on the veranda and the men settled themselves in comfy chairs, Phoebe distributed the soft drinks and joined Clarissa on a cushioned box seat.

Mum and Aunt Daphne had gone to the kitchen but I was still standing there, clutching my flowers, when I caught a look from the Fabulous Number Five and, suddenly flustered, said something about putting my beautiful flowers in water before they wilted in this dreadful heat. I had already crossed into the lounge room when I heard Number Five say he had better explain the food to the ladies, would my dad please excuse him, and suddenly he was right behind me.

All women who have ever fallen in love must feel that exquisitely sweet, painful, confusing lurch of one's insides. I felt it then for the first time ever. It's almost like being in a foreign country; suddenly the language is different, colours take on a different strength, there's music coming from nowhere and you want to dance. I was tinglingly conscious of his proximity and the dim knowledge that I had to pull myself together, be normal. Trouble was, I'd almost forgotten what normal meant.

At one o'clock, we sat down to a delicious lunch. The crispy spiced vegetables went beautifully with the turkey and the roasted veg and the boiled peas and cauliflower au gratin. We did the usual thing and pulled the crackers and put our hats on. The oldest of the Foreign Five looked a bit uncomfortable with his, which kept falling off. Dad told him he could leave it off but as Dad left his on I think our visitor thought he must keep his on, too, and manfully kept arranging it on his head. Whenever there was a lull in conversation, someone read the joke from his or her cracker which, for the most part, elicited derisive laughter.

We ascertained that Number Five had indeed cooked the food, to which he added that he thought the only reason the other four let him share the flat was because he could cook. Of course they protested, saying that all their families knew each other, did business together and the boys had promised to look after each other.

Number Five said, laughing, that he thought the other four had given up on him, to which one of them replied rather heatedly that Number Five was not living a proper Indian life, was not paying sufficient attention to his studies and spending too much time on other things. The last two words had dark overtones.

At that point, the oldest of our Indian visitors intervened and quietly reminded them to remember where they were and uttered a short word of apology to Dad. I could clearly see him, eventually, ruling his household with quiet authority; slippered feet on the polished floors, servants speaking in whispers, his wife and children a little bit in awe of him. And no sense of humour. Number Five beamed at everyone and said he was sorry, all his fault, made a joke at his own expense and we were back to the jolly party fare.

I think Christmas dinners are usually pretty long affairs and in the Queensland heat, probably even longer. By about two forty-five, we were considering dessert, which is practically another meal in itself, when the phone rang. I looked at my watch and thought, damn, Mum wondered who could be ringing at this time of day, Aunt asked the girls if they'd given the number to their friends, and Dad said he supposed someone should answer it and got up to do just that.

I was actually closest and normally did jump up to answer because often it was for me, so I got a funny look from Dad as he went by. My complexion was probably a bit pink, from guilt rather than liquid refreshment. I hadn't had much alcohol, anyway, as the spiciness of the Indian food had called for water rather than wine and while I had totally forgotten my ill-begotten plan ages back, at the beginning I had been conscious of having to drive later that day.

People used to stop talking altogether or at least lower their voices when someone was on the phone. I notice it doesn't happen so much now but I suppose then we thought the listener could better hear in surrounding silence. Today, people talk on their mobiles everywhere and strangers on the train or the bus or in a queue, or just walking in the street, aren't going to oblige by shutting up. Mind you, I often listen, because I'm nosey and you can get a lot of good ideas from a stray piece of conversation.

Anyway, on this occasion, everyone could hear Dad's end, so we all knew there'd been a fire in our rehearsal rooms, damaged props, and so on. and, yes, Dad was sure I'd go and help check out stuff and Dad hoped everything would be all right for the New Year's Eve panto.

I felt awful and could only utter a string of damns under my breath. The word perfidious comes to mind now; then, I thought how stupid could I get. The other members of the family wanted to know what had happened and our visitors were sympathetic to what sounded like some sort of tragedy. Well, tragedy it was. I was having fun and cursed myself for thinking up the stupid ruse in the first place. However, when Dad explained that Noel had said how sorry he was to drag me away from family and friends but he was trying to get as many as possible to go and help sort out what needed to be done – he didn't know the extent of the fire himself yet, he'd just had a call from the owners of the building, and so on and so on.

I said I'd better change my high-heeled sandals for something practical and Dad said I could borrow his car. Well, that was strange, because I hardly ever got to drive Dad's car, it was usually Mum's, but I was in no position to make any comment. If only Noel had just asked for me instead of blurting it out to Dad, I could have got out of it.

I made my apologies to everyone, saying how nice it had been to meet our visitors and hoped we'd meet again, the last being said as my eyes came to rest on Fab Number Five. Dad got his car keys and came out on to the veranda with me, quietly saying something about looking out for the other mad drivers on the road but I had an idea he thought my madness wasn't the same as other drivers' madnesses might be. Like I've said, Dad doesn't say much but he certainly seemed to have a sixth sense. Perceptive. Couldn't tell even the mildest fib to Dad, whereas Mum could easily be taken in.

Poor Phoebe had made things worse by asking if she could come with me. She was torn between her fascination with our visitors and her interest in theatre. I think, at school, it allowed her to give vent to her imagination. I truly felt awful but Dad, good old Dad, came to the rescue and vetoed it. I said I couldn't tell lies to him but on that occasion he certainly surprised me – he said that as the extent of the fire was unknown, he wouldn't take responsibility for Phoebe's safety

What do they say – have wheels, will travel? The problem was, where should I travel to? When I made this crazy arrangement with Noel, I hadn't actually thought that far ahead. I just wanted to escape what I thought was going to be a boring day. I started off in the general direction of the hall then thought I could go to the beach. Couldn't swim, of course, not being prepared, but it would be cool by the sea and I could paddle. I decided two hours away would do, the fire was minor and the others… No, better keep this between Noel and me, so poor Noel had to insist on taking any fire-smoked garments away with him to attend to. Yes, of course, dry-cleaning – he would take them to a cleaner near him that could, for a price, do overnight.

I was beginning to realise that it is, indeed, a tangled web we weave when we practise to deceive. One also needed a good memory and, if you don't believe it's easier to tell the truth than not, I'm telling you now.

By the time I got back home at nearly six, Foreign Five had left, the washing up was done and the family was comfortably sprawled on the veranda, catching the evening breeze.

I waved as I drove into the driveway and on into the garage by the side of the house. Dad got up and came down to meet me. Over loudly, I thought, he asked how things were and hoped they weren't too bad but as he took the car keys he leaned in closely and sniffed.

'Hmm,' he said quietly, 'smell more of sea salt than smoke.' But he put his arm around my shoulders and ushered me upstairs to the demands for information from the others.

I told them it was really minor, some fabrics had apparently caught fire from a stray, and illegal, firecracker, but they'd smouldered more than flamed and everything would be all right for the panto.

They wanted to know who had been able to get there and were most disappointed in the others that they'd left it to Noel and me. I said we'd managed it, and so on, and perhaps I could have a late dessert and would the others like something to nibble on, and no, no, I'd told them, I'll get it. I'm really not given to swearing but I must have thought or uttered more 'damns' in that afternoon than ever before or since.

I filled another jug of home-made lemonade and assembled an array of tasty snacks, plus my cold plum pudding and some halva, a semolina, spice and sultana concoction brought by our earlier visitors. Better enjoy this, I thought, because it's the last connection I'll ever have with Fab Number Five. Oh, I was kicking myself for having such a stupid idea as his image floated through my mind.

Aunt Daphne asked if we'd need to make any changes to our presentation because of costumes or props, Clarissa said she was looking forward to going, Mum reminded us all that Gran would be back and she was going too and wouldn't that be nice as she would then meet some of our visitors.

My ears had pricked up on that and as casually as I could, asked, 'How come?'

Mum told me that naturally they'd talked about the performance after I left and three had expressed an interest in seeing it.

'Oh,' I said, 'that's nice. Which three?'

Dad told me later that at the time I had a spoonful of dessert in my right hand but had reached over to get a piece of melon and salami with my left. He misses nothing. And I suppose he'd got into the habit of saying only what was absolutely necessary and at that moment my digestion was not one of them.

The cousins vied in telling which three, with many giggles, and it transpired that my Fab Number Five would be one of them. They also very kindly told me that in Indian culture only widows wore white; they'd been talking about the meaning of colours and the many borders on saris, each caste and area having different ones. All in all, I thought, I couldn't have had a more disastrous day.

The following days inched slowly by, notwithstanding visits to rehearsals and making sure everything was in order. I had to tell them what had happened and of course they thought it was a huge joke and that it could be the basis for a play. I told them to forget it and made them promise to back me up if necessary. As you can see, I didn't, still don't I hope, have a criminal mind because, if you think about it, such deception involves more than just the members of an amateur dramatics society. Who alerted the fire department, for instance? Have to say, though, I owe my dad heaps because on the night he really came up trumps – he kept the family, and the three young men who'd joined them, away from any cast or crew member, particularly Noel, and veered the conversation in a new direction if it looked like getting too close to that one.

The panto went well, finishing about ten p.m., which gave us time to clean up and get to our respective parties. Our extended family including Gran were going to the flat of Foreign Five. They'd invited a few more friends, so we were looking forward to meeting more people.

Mum and Dad had both taken their cars because of having the extra passengers of Aunt Daphne, Phoebe and Clarissa, and me after the show. The three young men left soon after the ending but not until they and Dad had persuaded Mum to follow with Gran, Aunt Daph and the girls. Dad would help clean up and take me.

Of course I had to come clean and while we were dismantling props I ventured that he knew, didn't he, that the fire fiasco was a complete fabrication. He agreed and was surprised that others hadn't seen through it, but never mind, if it was a secret, it was safe with him. He said that Noel, to his credit, was a bad liar and the firework and the smouldering was just too silly for words. It all sounded too contrived. Dad agreed that Mum could get carried away at times but even so, I was to watch myself, settle down and finish my studies and not get hurt by falling for the wrong or unattainable person. I said something to the effect that it might not be easy and Dad gave me a hug and said again to concentrate on my studies.

The party was in full swing but Fab Number Five came to us immediately we arrived. He took us to get drinks, introducing us along the way. I noticed Clarissa and Phoebe dancing merrily with each other, Aunt seemed to be in deep conversation with a young woman in a beautiful sari and Gran was on the sofa talking animatedly to two young teens. I heard my mum's voice somewhere but was glad to note that whoever those with her were, they had the temerity to interrupt her. Fab Number Five soon had Dad ensconced in conversation with an older fellow, now resident here with his family, and I was whisked off to dance.

At some point, I asked if he liked cricket. He was a bit evasive but when pressed had to admit it was not his favourite pastime. I asked what was and he said he really liked messing about with lighting and had, in fact, done the town's lighting when the Queen had visited Fiji. He was fourteen at the time. I told him how pleased I was to hear all of that. I asked him what he'd thought of the pantomime and he said he'd only ever heard of Punch and Judy so he was a bit surprised by ours, although the idea behind it seemed the same. He wondered if perhaps he could join the drama society I belonged to and perhaps help with lighting and stuff. I teased, and said that the uni had its own, he could join that, but when he looked so disappointed, I relented and said I was sure we could use him. The way I was feeling, I could have promised him anything. At midnight he kissed me.

You don't need me to tell you the rest of the story. It wasn't plain sailing; he was loosely connected with a girl back home and her family created a fuss. His own family wasn't too bad but were naturally concerned by the differences in culture. After we'd been going out together for about two years and we knew what we wanted, his mum and dad made a trip over.

They stayed with my mum and dad, who had really been comfortable with the whole thing once they saw we were serious. That helped win his folks over, except for one of his sisters. She has never really come over to our side and, while we visit each other, I feel there isn't a total thaw. Some of his Indian friends in Brisbane tut-tutted a bit but I'm happy to say they all came to the wedding. Most of my friends were pleased for us but, like his, some had their reservations.

We each finished our studies and now he's a professor at a Sydney university and I teach drama at a secondary school. I also do programmes at a youth detention centre and am currently looking into working with refugees. Most people are amused but don't know why I call my beautiful husband Chanel and why, every New Year, I'm given a bottle of Chanel No. Five. I did learn how to elegantly wear a sari, which I'd put on if I was with his parents. Phoebe became a theatre director and Clarissa is a doctor.

We have two beautiful sons, whom their grandparents take off to play or watch cricket. We don't mind, because that's where my story started; and is it or is it not, cricket?

Monologue

Pieces of unattached quilting, meant to be something; unfinished tapestries that never reach the wall. A multi-thousand-piece jigsaw puzzle that looks as if it's coming together then someone, something, causes it to fall and once again it's in little pieces on the floor. That's my life.

So I scrabble about, collect the bits, hoping none is lost, and try to start again. Each time is more difficult than the last. I've given up on the more textured stuff; unruffled two-dimensional will have to do. Have to do – it would be heaven if I could only get it together. I started out as a free agent, no strings attached. Well, that's a funny one. There was one string, pre-birth, but cut that and you're on your own. Things have come a long way in my lifetime, babies created in Petri dishes, IVF and what not, but not when I was born. And still, for the baby to survive, it does become attached, pre-birth. But babies used to be conceived in the 'natural' way. Is it still that, with other ways becoming so commonplace? I wonder how those children feel? I mean, I wasn't contrived, I just wasn't wanted.

Mostly we applaud medical science advances, but is this an advance? Personally I'd prefer they concentrated on curing diseases. They could start with the common cold, though I don't know what's so common about it now, there are so many strains – or is that flu? – but anyway, everyone gets something like it. Often regularly. I mean, if a woman can't have children naturally, is she really suited for motherhood? Ah, you say, what if it's the man; what if his sperm isn't vigorous enough or something? I suppose it helps if doctors can get the two together, sperm and egg I mean, but what about when donor sperm is used? How do you know that he or she isn't your half-sibling you've fallen in love with because there are so many things each admires in the other. Narcissus. Well, I know I'm not related to anyone else.

But can I say that categorically? I know the mater didn't try it again but the pater – well, I don't know. Maybe that's why I never get it together. I keep falling in love with bits of myself and nature needs difference. Doesn't it? Ah well, I didn't perpetuate my line, as they say, so that's the end of that. No grief for anyone close to me. Maybe that's my gift to the world. But that's ridiculous – you can't make a gift of a vacuum.

I might have been unwanted but my parents had consciences. They weren't married to each other, which might have been why I didn't have a home, but on my good days I used to think that maybe they loved each other. Their histories are rather vague. One thinks of home as family but of course I did have a home, my own private little orphanage. I lived with a nanny, a carer, housekeeper, call her what you will. As she grew older, little things would slip out and I'd add them to my little store of things – the distorted facts I believed, the things I wanted to believe, the difficulty in separating the stuff of imagination from the factual. At some stage, even little girls growing up in happy families with siblings often believe themselves to be adopted. They dream of the parents they think they'd like to have, how life would be so different if only…

My companion and I lived in a flat, apartment, in the centre of town. At five, I started school, a costly one I learned later but not one I found overly friendly. It might have been my fault as much as anyone else's; I mean, I didn't really have any clues about making friends and my education had started years before. It wasn't my fault that my reading, writing, maths skills were so far ahead of my age group. I also spoke Spanish and French as well as English. I'd had nothing else to do. I continued to excel, kept up with the languages, for which I was thankful later.

Here, this is me, all those years ago. You can see the looseness in my stockings, there, around my ankles. Narrow ankles, narrow feet. Everything else was made to measure. I loved that coat, navy with tartan lining and the detailed stitching. Can you still get children's clothing like that? The winter dress underneath was tartan with navy collar and cuffs, long sleeves, yoke with box pleats and a loose belt. Those shoes are back in fashion, court with a narrow strap over the instep. Perhaps they've never been out of it.

It took about eighteen months but I did make one friend, then another. They were happy times, laughing times. I'd laughed before but at different things. I suppose I was lucky Nanny knew about humour. Had a sense of. But it was adult – I was old long before my time. It was inevitable I had to wait to become an adult before I came into my own. Well, it's that way for everyone but normal people evolve, don't they? Go through stages, phases, carve out who they are. I arrived, fully formed as an intellectual being; I just had to wait for my body to catch up.

I studied political science and became a diplomat. Well, you can see, can't you, I would be suited for something like that. By accident or design I was a private person, not given to sharing confidences. According to my measure of things, my life had, before this, had its high points but diplomacy is a different country altogether. It might be likened to Holly- or Bollywood; they're not real either. One is forever being debriefed. The people one meets, likes, maybe falls in love with – well, who are they? Is it a role they're playing or are they being real? Do they know? Some liken it to playing a game: rules are followed and at the end of a certain time, the whistle blows, the player packs up his, her, kit and goes home. I stayed on because it was my life. Excuse me, I have to laugh; you've no idea of the subterfuge; the news one reads, hears, is only a minute fraction of what could be told.

But it did come to an end as all things must. I retired. But retired to what? At school, university, I'd been interested in drama – well, there you are, you see, play-acting. That's all I've ever done. I thought of travelling to places I hadn't been to during my career but it didn't appeal. I frittered for what seems a long time. I still live in the apartment but Nanny, of course, is long-since dead. I rattle around in it by myself. I deal with the same firms Nanny did but it seems to me there's not the same willingness, somehow. It's either they think they're doing one a favour or they resent one. Perhaps it's the same thing. These days one has to do more for oneself, I think. Perhaps that's not a bad thing.

My first school is still operating. Changed, though. The uniform is basically the same but the little girls who chatter by are often wearing quite ornate jewellery in their ears. We were never allowed anything like that, couldn't even wear a wristwatch until our senior years. They've admitted boys to the junior classes. It's not that I spend my time spying out of the window, I wouldn't want you to think that, but their high-pitched little voices attract one's attention and I do take pleasure in seeing their happy faces. Occasionally there's a little girl, or a boy, dragging along, alone. I wonder about their families, all of them, extroverts and the quiet ones. I did meet my parents, separately, a few years ago. It wasn't anything, really, no spark, no basis for a friendship, any sort of relationship. Are parents and children friends, become friends as they age?

I feel for those little lost ones.

A few weeks ago, a leaflet was put through my door. Normally I would throw it out but I caught sight of the school's logo at the top. I was surprised at the drop in standards, delivering leaflets like this. I mean, it's so common. But I read it. Well, things have changed, they want volunteers to help with slow learners. Well, I was going to put the leaflet in the bin then but I didn't. It stayed on the bench top. It was there every morning when I made my tea and toast. Finally, I thought, well, I wonder… I walked along to the school, it's two blocks from my flat. No one there from my time, of course, but my name was there on the honour board.

I go now on Mondays and Thursdays. Sometimes it's just one to one, other times I have two, three, together. They're coming along beautifully. On other days, I watch them from my window; they all wave whether or not I have them for our little get-togethers. Next term we're starting a drama class. I'm so looking forward to it.

You'll have to excuse me now. I have a tapestry to finish. Historical;
it will make a good backdrop.

Heroes

She stood on my doorstep, tall, angular, in an all-enveloping too-large navy overcoat altogether too heavy for the season.

'Oh hi,' I said, 'you must be Thea. I'm… I've been expecting you. Come in.'

I invited Thea to remove her coat but she declined so I suggested I show her around the house and the painting that needed to be done. I was renovating an old house – I should say, I was having an old house renovated as I'd found I could do little of the work myself and employing others. Thea had been referred to me, a retired social worker, by her case worker as someone who knew all about paint. I explained what needed to be done and discussed payment and my plight of not having a lot of cash at my disposal. Thea's contribution to the conversation was occasional mumbled monosyllables.

The case worker had given me the information I needed – Thea was forty-two, had been married and had two just-teen children. She had recently come out and admitted to her part of the world that she was transgender. The only people in that small world who continued to love and care about her were her children.

Thea took the job and turned up each day, apart from the days she needed to see one or other of her medical team. Initially she refused to stop work to share morning coffee with me, so I would make her a drink and something to nibble on and just leave it in the vicinity of where she was working. I kept on asking her and finally told her she was being mean in denying me the pleasure of conversation. We started to become friends; I told her bits of my life and she began telling me bits of hers. Her knowing, at the age of two or three, that she was in the wrong body; she wasn't a boy, she was a girl; the running, the hiding, the teasing, the loneliness. The theft, and hiding, of her sister's silky garments and the beating she'd received when her father found her in one of her sister's frocks.

Coming from a working-class family, she was pushed into a trade, became a motor vehicle spray painter, couldn't evade the drinks at the pub with workmates and survival, self-preservation meant having a girlfriend. She was married at twenty-one and eventually two children were produced, after which sexual intercourse virtually ceased. But twenty-one years after marriage, she decided she really would succeed with suicide or come out.

As she painted her way around the inside of my house and various visitors came, Thea would make her long frame as small as possible in whatever corner she was working in. I would introduce her as my super-clever painter and my guests would say hello to her upturned bottom if she was working on skirting boards, or otherwise just her back. I told her there was nothing wrong with her front and it was much nicer to talk to but knew it was going to take time in this small community.

Thea was still working for me when the first anniversary of my being in the house rolled around. I invited something like eighty friends to a garden party, Thea included.

She arrived early but once others began to arrive, she sought to hide away. We'd already discussed the value in meeting people, people she didn't know from her former life, so I found her and gave her a job of passing trays of food around. Many friends commented on the great job she was doing with my painting because of course I had advertised her skills, which were considerable. One of my guests had broken her leg very badly and recognised Thea as the taxi driver she regularly asked for; my friend said Thea was the most careful driver and very solicitous in helping my friend in and out of the cab, and carrying shopping or anything else to where my friend wanted it in her home.

Thea later took a job as a carer in an older persons' home, her highlight taking a group out on picnics. People previously strangers were accepting Thea for who she was, valuing her as a person.

By this time, we'd advanced to the stage at which we could talk about past and present lives, check the changes in her body as the injected hormones started and would continue to soften her features, change her shape. Thea was having difficulty in accepting the loss of muscle strength she'd previously had but enjoyed the loss of hair on her body and she'd joke about the competition with her growing daughter, regarding the development of their relevant bosoms.

We would spend a lot of time discussing her relationship with her mother, her former wife, her siblings. Thea would be upset when one or the other lapsed and called her by her first given name and I told the story of my sister who had done nothing more than change her name simply because she didn't like it and the problems the rest of our family had in always remembering the new, longer, version of her original. And of course Thea's family would refer to events in her past life, as we all do, but Thea no longer lived there and wanted no reminders of it.

I encouraged Thea to try to look at things from the others' point of view, particularly her former wife and the concerns she might feel for her growing children. Did Thea think, for instance, her former wife might question her own judgement? She had fallen in love with and married someone who was not who she thought he was. Could she trust anyone, in any circumstance, ever again?

Of course her mother had difficulty in accepting this new person, one sister was quicker than the other and her brother remained antagonistic, though her sister-in-law was more accepting. I hope she was able to work on her husband. I can imagine the lewd sexual conversations that would have taken place at the pub with her brother and mates, and now one of their own had 'gone over to the other side'.

I welcomed her children. Those two teenagers were, in their own way, heroes, loving and standing up for the person who had been their father and was now Thea.

My admiration for her, Thea, will never waver. I believe it is more difficult to come out at an older age but she took that step and with the support of homosexual/transgender groups, medicos, new friends she started making a new life for herself. We talked about it and held her hands when it was time to go interstate for the big op. We helped with funds for her daughter to go with her the first time and made a fuss of her when she returned.

By this time, Thea had formed a relationship with another woman. Sally is a musician, lots of fun, and had had her eye on Thea for some time. In many ways, this relationship was good for Thea – someone really loved her, wanted her as a partner, but I'll never really know if it was the right thing for her. She had spoken about having a relationship with a man; hadn't seen herself as a lesbian, though many of her friends were. I have a sneaking suspicion Thea would wish she'd had the opportunity of a male-female relationship. She was of course, still very fragile; I wonder if anyone, having made such a huge change in a life, is ever, wholly, totally, psychologically healthy.

Thea and Sally moved to a tiny remote village where they were totally unknown and Thea's relationship with me slowly came to an end. I am sorry about that. I think part of the reasoning behind the move was to spare her family any ongoing embarrassment and for Thea herself, who was increasingly feeling fully female emotions – quick to tears, that sort of thing, and her embarrassment over that. She needed somewhere to get to know herself. She would have to travel back to the metropolis for medical treatment but no one needed to know. She could be anonymous in the city.

It is true, we cannot fully appreciate what anyone is experiencing unless we walk in their shoes. Through my relatively brief relationship with Thea, I gained much knowledge and insight into her physical and psychological well-being and, by extension, that of others in a similar position. This does not make me an expert and I would not presume to claim that but I do feel easier when speaking with members of the LGBTI community. My friends have always included male homosexual people, not so many female ones.

Thea taught me much, for which I thank her.

Musical Reverie

'Listen, do you hear that? What is that music? Just the first three or four notes remind me of a Tibetan horn. I can see the player, now, standing in bright woven shawls contrasting against the sharp, peaked, white slopes of the mountains. The horn was longer than his height was tall. Such echoing sound, each note hitting, rebounding from each surface. Each echo answered by sun-bright snow crystals. Diamond sound.

'Oh, now it's a 1920s dance tune. It's 1927 and I'm thirteen years old. I'd been allowed to sit up in the balcony and watch the ball below. The sleekly brilliant heads atop stiff white shirt fronts backed by black tails contrasting with their light as a feather, beaded, sequinned, lace-layered partners. The clothes almost epitomised the insubstantiality of the wearers. Like butterflies, and with little more thought. At that age, I hadn't begun to think, really think, and I had no idea what went on in the heads of people six or more years older than I. Peacock feathers, I remember, fashioned into handbags or part of a dress decoration.

'That same shimmering, rich colour was at my sister's wedding. But not in feathers; oh, yes, it was the dress: a taffeta that was bronze-gold, turquoise, copper, deep red, all at once or just a hint depending on the light or the way the wearer moved. I was eighteen then and about to go up to Oxford. So many changes in that time. I had more choices but the old glamour was gone.

'There'd been the Crash of '29 three years before. Some of our friends were still recovering their losses; some never did. It had been a registry office wedding with a small reception for a hundred up at the house. My sister. Her wedding. I was very happy then. The spires of Oxford, almost mystical when one saw them from a distance through the mist. The peaks of the Himalayas were grand, frightening in a way but the spires of Oxford beckoned. I was looking forward to starting my studies in history and English literature but I remember chiding my brother – how old was he then, let me think, twenty-six, and my sister would have been twenty-four. Why was I cross with him?

'Oh, yes, he had joined in the conversation with some of the older men and it was all Adolf Hitler and Europe and the probability of war. All of our conversations seemed to be of war: the Great War, the Spanish war. Older men who had been part of the Great War had come back with stories of horror. My uncle, Mama's brother, had come back traumatised and was institutionalised. Some of my brother's friends had come back from Spain damaged in mind or body. I just reminded them they were at a wedding and let it drop for a while. When I think back to that ball, it had been to announce the engagement of the Hon. Hermione Somebody-or-other to the son of friends of my parents. I hardly knew them, but I think they were embracing life with a passion they didn't understand themselves. As it happened, so many of them had so much life to live in such a short time. So many of those young men had such short lives. Women, too. Such a waste.

I ended up in London about 1941. For a time, I'd tutored at Oxford but one day I was invited to tea with the dean. It was all so cloak and dagger, a bit of a giggle now, but so hush-hush then. I'd been recommended for a job in 'Somebody's Office', no names, just 'so terribly important' and the dean, so solemn, said I should very seriously think about it. Much more valuable there, he'd said, than here, although they'd miss me, of course, et cetera. Of course it was exciting but awful, too. Near daily bombings, death and destruction everywhere. Children being made orphans or quasi-orphans when they were sent away to Ireland, Wales, English countryside.

My brother was in the RAF. He'd always loved flying and I had a young man, also in the air force. My brother-in-law was an engineer working somewhere in England. Neither my brother nor my young man would marry Sophie or me. Said it was better to wait until after the war. I could see the sense of that; the responsibility of one might affect the responsibility of the other. And my young man and I weren't exactly innocents when it came to the physical side of things.

'They were both dead by August 1943. Poor Mama. Poor Papa, too. Sophie took it very badly. She married when she was about fifty; I think they've been happy. I hope so. One should at least expect to be happy. Live in Lincoln, now. Must write. I wish I'd become pregnant; I was left with nothing. I didn't want to live without Robert. They managed to let me have two or three days off work but really, everyone was needed at their posts. I think I worked like an automaton. No time or energy to be angry or sad and there was no funeral to go to. Memorial services, not quite the same. I used to see his face, suddenly, in a crowd, and my heart would leap in happy anticipation but then I would be plunged again into black despair when I realised it wasn't him. Or I'd rush up to someone whose back, way of walking, was just like his. It was an awful time. I still see him in my mind, laughing, bright blue eyes, young. Youth, forever held in the few photographs, taken here, mostly, at the house. And I'm an old woman.

'The house had been made over into a hospital by then. I'd manage to get home every now and then and there'd be broken and burnt men sitting on this very bench or in wheelchairs scattered about the lawns. I don't know what kind of life they had to look forward to but somebody must have loved them and some life must be better than no life at all.

'Before the war, we all used to get home fairly often. I remember one particular time when my sister, I think, had brought up the subject of Jewish refugees and that perhaps a good part of the house could be made over to housing some of them. Dear Mama wasn't sure and wanted to know how European Jews might differ from English Jews. I suppose we had Jewish friends if I remember the names. The Goldsteens and Fabers used to come in to play cards.

'My sister was cross and said that at least they wouldn't eat the pigs and Mama and Papa could eat pork chops for the duration of the war.

Everyone laughed, except poor Mama, who looked so hurt. But then she went on to say about how she was losing domestic staff to better-paid jobs in factories and three-fourths of the house was both unused and getting very dusty, so she supposed it would be all right and we all tried hard to suppress another outburst of laughter.

'In the end, it was better to have it used as the hospital. Mama and Papa were involved in various ways and used to arrange for entertainers to come up. Some of them were Jewish refugees; they used to play the violin. Such sad, plaintive music, but then they'd change to fast dance music. Their own dances. Italian farm workers played accordions. Some would sing pieces of opera. Always quick to smile and they loved children. They'd bring out photographs of their own little ones. It seemed hard to remember, sometimes, that they were the enemy. Such a waste, war.

'My work had nothing to do with children but it's the children I think of most. So innocent. The war had nothing to do with them. I got a job with the United Nations not long after it was formed. Had some help from university fellows and my London contacts. As soon as the Children's Emergency Fund started, I transferred to that. That was how I was able to travel as I did. I saw some appalling sights but I'll never stop being amazed by the children. So resilient. Physical injuries, the loss of an arm or leg, didn't stop them from laughing, joining in the games. And they all played games, with whatever was at hand. They made music, too, out of all sorts of things. Drums were easy but they'd somehow persuaded one of the men to drill holes in a precious piece of pipe, stones in a tin.

'People would sing as they went about making new lives for themselves. Often they had no homes and the homes that there were often were without water or electricity. Everyone worked to try to get back to some sort of normalcy. Rubble was everywhere and every so often a part of a human skeleton would emerge. Small children were just curious but it would send reverberations throughout the adults, stirring up the recent emotions of having buried their own dead, mourning with those whose loved ones had not been found. There'd be the processes of identification, and a heaviness descended on the people. I remember the eyes of some of the young adults, still children really, but made old long before their time. They'd witnessed horrors no one should ever see, or do, if we are ever to call ourselves a civilised people. It makes me so angry.

'Of course the images changed as I continued with my work and travel. African children so different from South American children but their needs are the same. Good food, education, stability. A family to love them. We owe them that.

'Everyone has music, you know, of one sort or another. A hollowed sapling, strings attached to a board, little pipes, bells of different sizes and sound. So important in people's lives. Church bells; are they church bells I can hear? The first time I saw the campanile in St Mark's Square and the mosaics. So rich; so intricate, pictures in coloured bits of tile. I love the Christmas tunes played by the bell ringers. Bells are part of Indian life too. The rainbow-sari-clad dancers strap rows of tiny bells around their ankles and they make such a noise when you can hardly see their feet, they are moving so quickly. They have different kinds of drums and a sort of accordion and a beautiful stringed instrument. Some of them were very good singers, too. That was where a little group of village children presented me with a bouquet of peacock feathers. Some were already old, dusty, broken. But so precious. I wonder where they are now?'

'That's the house bell, Auntie. My Emily and George must have made tea. Do you still have Robert's photos, Auntie? I've never seen any. Was he really handsome and didn't you want to fall in love again?'

'Dear children. Not really children any more. They must have been playing the music that set me off on this long reverie. My sister. Of course, she's your mother. Sorry, darling. I suppose I've been talking out loud? So many memories and I get so tired. All young people with a purpose are handsome. And I was too busy for anyone else; Robert was the only one and in a sense I felt I was carrying on his work – making peace, providing opportunity for ordinary people. There's that bell, again, and what is that music?'

'I don't know. We'll ask George. But come on, they'll have prepared a lovely tea and then your energy will be restored and you can tell more stories. Perhaps a change of music will send you down a different track.'

Indian Holiday

My friend and I were on holiday in India, at this point travelling by bus from Jumna to Kashmir. We'd been in Jumna, a dusty, busy, colourful town, for a few days, staying in what once might have been a minor palace. Now it was a very roughly divided hotchpotch of suites or apartments. Our apartment had a beautiful bathroom, however, with the biggest, deepest marble bath. Like everything else, it needed cleaning but I floated in that bath thinking of the history it had lent itself to. The intrigues, the romance.

As I bumped along in the bus, wondering how it was going to stay together, I tried not to think of my own structure. My knees were almost under my chin, for lack of space, and I was sure that every joint that could be dislocated would be. My friend sat sideways, legs in the aisle, leaning on me. We agreed the driver's name must be Schumacher's brother, the slow one.

Our fellow passengers, locals all, seemed able to tuck themselves away, for all I could see in the dim light that came back from the weak yellow headlights were what looked like mounds of roughly sorted laundry. We climbed upwards, the road narrow and potholed, with soaring rock almost grazing one side, on the other nothing. Apart from the straining of the bus, all was quiet and dark.

Suddenly our world was flooded with light. A car was stopped in the middle of the road ahead. Two dark figures were waving their arms at the bus as it shuddered to a stop. The mounds were instantly alert but made no sound only to quiet the small children who had wakened. Quickly and silently, any jewellery that had slipped out from between the folds of their garments was pushed back in, parcels slid under the seats. Apart from watches, my friend and I wore no jewellery and our luggage was on the roof of the bus. We had already experienced bandits on a train in central India so were fairly philosophical about losing our possessions but here, the political situation was rather delicate, so anything could happen.

The figures, male, boarded the bus, saying something to the driver, who just seemed to shrink into himself. My friend and I were near the front and must have been instantly recognisable as foreigners but one of the men made his way along the cramped aisle to the back. In dialect, he brusquely addressed seven or eight passengers, who muttered in reply. As he made his way down again, I sensed an unrest, a slight rumbling; all eyes were turned upon us as he stopped at our seat. The other man was standing on the steps.

Somewhere between a request and an order, in passable English, we were told to leave the bus. We had our passports on us and our respective High Commissions had been given our itineraries. However, if we disappeared, the authorities wouldn't know of it for some time and could then only trace our movements backwards. During which time anything could have happened and we could be anywhere. Do we brazen it out, insist on our being allowed to peacefully continue on our journey or get off? Understandably, the locals didn't want, or deserve, any trouble and the feelings towards us now were those of hostility. My friend and I made eye contact and it was understood we'd get off. Once off, the driver was ordered to unload our luggage. The poor man appeared terrified and avoided looking at us.

We and our bags were quickly bundled into the car, which I now noticed still had its engine running. It shot forward quicker than any speed driver. We tried to wriggle to some comfortable place between the broken springs, at the same time checking out our abductors, the interior of the car – door locks, et cetera, and tried with our feet to find any loose hard object on the floor.

When the road had widened somewhat and we could have hurled ourselves out of the car without hitting the cliff or falling off it, I summoned my best British voice and, with a modicum of authority, demanded to know what they thought they were doing.

The two turned around, teeth gleaming in a wide grin. 'Good joke, eh. What you think? Oh, ho ho, those puny villagers think you are spies. Very afraid. They said, "Take them, take them."'

'And now you have taken us, what do you intend?'

'We own your houseboat. Didn't want you to travel in that uncomfortable dirty old bus,' came the reply.

Under the Umbrella

There's always a feeling of peace in Graeme's garden. It's not tidy, it's rather wild in fact, but perhaps that's the attraction to the many birds and butterflies that frequent it. The flowers impart a feeling of exuberance and the bright, giant Nepali umbrella almost becomes one of them.

We'd spent most of the day there while the girls were away playing tennis, talking of everything but our future. We recognised the need to recharge our batteries, so we relaxed. I'd made a fresh pot of tea when we heard car doors slamming, the girls shouting thanks and farewells to their friends.

They came straight through to the garden. Healthy, bright-looking girls, skins aglow with youth and high spirits. Elizabeth, sure of herself at seventeen and the thorn in my side and her father's . It was to his side that she flew, flinging herself to sit on the armrest of his chair, her arm possessively thrown around Graeme's neck, plunging into the excitements of her day while my greetings and her father's were lost in the torrent. As usual, my presence was ignored.

At fourteen, Nancy was still finding herself. She loved her father no less than did Elizabeth but she couldn't cope with the atmosphere created by her sister. Graeme, Nancy and I got on beautifully together. It was almost with reluctance that she trailed after Elizabeth to join the now uneven group.

'Hello, Daddy. Hello, Janet,' she said, kissing first me and then Graeme then standing disconsolately, eclipsed by Elizabeth's volubility.

'I'm glad you've had a good day, Elizabeth, but calm down for a moment, will you?' Graeme said, untangling himself from his elder daughter's grasp. 'How about you, Nancy, did you have a good day, too?'

'Oh, yes, it was all right but I need to improve my game a lot,' she was saying when Elizabeth broke in, saying disparagingly, 'Yes, Brent was there, so she made a mess of all her serves.'

Nancy coloured and I put my hand out to catch hold of hers. 'Never mind, Nancy, my game could do with some improvement; how about we work on it together?'

As if I hadn't spoken, Elizabeth said, 'You'll have to play more with Nancy, Daddy. She is so clumsy.'

'Janet's just said she'll play more with Nancy. We can't both run the poor girl ragged, can we, sweetie?' Graeme said, looking fondly at his younger daughter.

Elizabeth just tossed her head. I still wasn't there as far as she was concerned. I said I'd go and get some more refreshments and cool drinks and rose to head for the kitchen. It seemed Elizabeth and I just couldn't share the same space. Her father and I had been friends for more than a year, having met in a travel agency. He was booking a skiing trip for himself and the girls; I was looking at brochures of Nepal. Graeme noticed and remarked how lovely it was. We started talking about travel, where we'd each been until Graeme said why didn't we chat more comfortably over a coffee? We finalised our respective business and went to the nearest coffee shop.

Graeme told me he'd been a widower for more than a year. It had been a good marriage, happy and very lucky in many ways, two beautiful daughters, no financial problems, holidays to interesting parts of the globe. He missed his wife, the children their mother, but he and his younger daughter, Nancy, seemed to realise that life went on and should be embraced. Elizabeth, on the other hand, seemed to be angry all the time and was really possessive of him.

I murmured how difficult that would be and general enquiries about extended family support. I continued that I also had lost my partner, but five years ago, and while time does make it easier, of course I missed those moments of intimacy and easy banter. My son, John, was at university and seemed to live half at home, half somewhere else. It transpired we were both working in education, I lecturing on textiles, Graeme teaching English and history at a high school. Our workplaces were on opposite sides of town but we had some acquaintances in common. Our conversation had to come to an end; I had things to do and that evening John was home for dinner. Graeme asked if we could meet again and we arranged to have lunch at the same place the following week.

We met more often. Graeme thought it was time I met his girls so I was invited to afternoon tea. It was a beautiful summer day, just right under the umbrella. Nancy was friendly but Elizabeth was hostile.

We'd been trying for a flow of conversation for a while when Elizabeth suddenly said, 'This is Mummy's umbrella. We don't normally allow strangers under it.'

Graeme asked what on earth she was going on about, it was everybody's umbrella, friends often sat under it, Elizabeth was being rude and should apologise. Elizabeth shouted that her father had no business inviting me and how could he do this to her mother. At which point she'd turned and fled into the house.

Graeme looked at me in shocked silence then, getting up, said how sorry he was but he must go and speak with Elizabeth. I agreed, said I would leave, maybe we could talk soon. As he made his way to the house, I collected my bag, took out my car keys. Poor Nancy had been quite forgotten but I did see her then. She was so pale, poor thing, and her eyes were brimming with unshed tears. It was a natural thing to put my arms around her. I tried to say a few comforting words but said that I must go, and she should join her family.

Graeme and I continued seeing each other and I was invited back to the house, but Elizabeth always managed to be on the point of going somewhere or had already left. Our meetings were like passing ships in the night.

Poor Elizabeth, I thought now, as I put scones into the microwave, she really is so afraid of losing her one remaining parent. What can I do to convince her I don't want to take Graeme away, but for them, all three, to accept me?

Nancy broke in on my reverie as I was filling the jam and cream dishes.

'Can I help you, Janet?' she asked, looking no happier than she had outside. 'I can't stand the way Elizabeth is,' she blurted, 'Mummy's been dead more than two years now and I don't think she'd want us to be all alone. We had a lot of fun before she got sick. We used to laugh all the time, even when she was sick she could still share jokes and see the funny side of things and make us see them too. You'd have been friends if you'd known her.' She stopped suddenly, her hand flying to her mouth, eyes wide open, looking at me, stricken, 'Oh, Janet, I didn't mean to say that, you know, I mean…' and two tears rolled down her face.

'Oh, Nancy,' I hugged her, 'I know what you mean. You know, if I had met all of you before your mother died, I think we would have been friends, too. Your daddy and I wouldn't have fallen in love with each other because we would have been different people then. Different circumstances cause us to behave in different ways. And even though your mum isn't here now, I think she and I are still friends in a sort of a way, because she is part of you and Elizabeth and so much of your father's life. I think Elizabeth is unhappy because she might feel a bit, you know, disloyal or something, if she lets herself like me or considers her father is replacing her mother. But it's nothing like that. When people leave our lives, they don't take away what they gave us, and when people come into our lives, they give more, add to what we have already.' I gave her a squeeze and asked if she was feeling better. 'Okay,' I said, 'do you want to just get out a couple of glasses for juice and we'll take this into the garden?'

We returned to the umbrella.

As Graeme rose to take the tray, his look clearly said, 'What are we going to do?'

All I could manage was a slight shrug and small grimace.

Once Graeme had put the tray down, I announced it was time I was going. I did have things to do and couldn't cope with another session of the not-there treatment from Elizabeth. Only Nancy replied to my farewells and hopes for a good week at school.

Graeme accompanied me to my car. 'What are we going to do, Janet? I've talked to her, told her I don't love her mother any less, which you know and understand. I explained we have to move on and I love you and oh, how I want us to share our lives, Janet, and just be a family again. I could be talking to a brick wall. Nancy is unhappy. They're not getting on – I suppose there's a difference between being seventeen and nearly adult, though you wouldn't believe it right now, and fourteen, which I suppose is just on the first steps to getting there.'

'Well, we could marry anyway,' I replied, taking his hand, 'but only if you stop banging on my car. Seriously, we have to sort it out. No good starting on the wrong foot. We could try another round table discussion, although the last was a disaster and I vowed and declared I wouldn't do it again. Leave it for the moment, darling. Go and share another scone with them. I'll see you at lunch tomorrow as usual.'

We kissed goodbye and I was in my car and down the driveway before he had time to get back to the girls.

What a problem, I thought, as I drove. John doesn't mind – in fact, he couldn't be happier. Perhaps sons are different, especially sons who have already left home. He'd met Graeme several times but declined to meet the girls until we had sorted things out. Said he didn't want to complicate things by being either the horrible stepbrother-to-be or one – or, heaven help us, both – of the girls getting a crush on him. 'Just let me know when the wedding is and I'll gladly walk you to the altar, or whatever you want.' he said.

'Oh, John,' I said in mock alarm, 'you're not giving me away, are you? You don't feel I'm deserting you or anything, do you, darling?'

'Oh, Mum, come on. You've been on your own for too long already. And if you leave it any longer, you'll be old and grey and toothless and no one will have you.' At which point he did what all good cricketers do and caught the cushion I'd hurled at him. 'Seriously, though, Mum, Graeme's a nice bloke. I think you've done a pretty good job on your own. It couldn't have been easy sometimes. And if you've found someone you want to spend whatever time with and be happy, that's okay by me. Here endeth the lesson.' And he threw the cushion back.

Life went on as usual, no solution in sight.

One lunchtime, Graeme reported on a conversation he had unashamedly listened to from outside the bathroom. The door was slightly ajar and Elizabeth had shouted at Nancy for going in. Nancy screamed how much she hated Elizabeth, how unfair she was, and she knew, though she was only fourteen, that one day she and Elizabeth would leave home and what would I do then? I'd be an old man and all alone. 'Had to smile at that,' Graeme said. 'She obviously doesn't put me in the too old basket right now, but she went on to ask Elizabeth if she ever thought how generous their mother had been and if Elizabeth really loved her, she should try to copy her. She's fourteen, for goodness sake! What a wise head on such young shoulders.'

'And what did Elizabeth say to all that?'

'The usual non-answer of youth – "Oh, what do you know about it?" at which point I disappeared into my room.'

A few weeks later, Graeme was quieter, more thoughtful.

'What is it?' I asked.

'Well, Elizabeth, actually,' he replied, 'I took her a cup of hot chocolate last night while she was doing her homework. She had books on divorce and reconstituted families lying about. I asked her what it was about. She said they'd had a visit from someone at one of those family counselling places. They'd discussed the high rates of divorce, how children feel about it, how it might affect them, and now she was writing about it.'

'That's interesting.' I couldn't help a wry grin. 'How was she taking it?'

'Quieter than usual. She seemed to have thought about what she was reading and writing,' Graeme replied slowly, trying not to look too hopeful. 'As if I had never said anything on the subject before, I remarked that it appeared to be a fairly common phenomenon these days and that maybe she'd care to discuss our situation. I made no reference to previous discussions, most of them aborted as you know, but this time she said okay, not exactly with great eagerness, but at least she agreed so I thought, you know, let's rush in where angels fear… How about Saturday?'

Of course I agreed. It would be nice if I could say that everything was sorted right then, but I can't. We were, however, able to talk more objectively, more honestly. Over the following weeks, we discussed divorce, death of a partner, then our own situation. We started going out together, mostly the four of us, but John has joined us for the odd meal. I thought we were making real progress when Elizabeth casually asked if we'd like to go the school art show first night! Bring John, too, she'd said. I think it gives her some cachet with her girlfriends to have a good-looking older male somehow connected to her.

She's unsure sometimes about 'loyalty' – is she betraying her mother? Then she might suddenly withdraw, but we're able to talk about that too. She understands her father mightn't want to spend his life without a partner. Nancy is happy as can be. She just wants life to be simple and happy.

Eight months have gone. I've finished sewing the girls' dresses and Graeme will be arriving with them, the girls, any minute. They're staying with me tonight. Elizabeth has taken on the role of chief attendant and, among other things, has to paint our fingernails with the apricot polish she scoured the city for. It's a paler shade of their dresses. After she'd seen my outfit, she discussed styles with Nancy and they'd agreed apricot would suit them both. Sweet Nancy is bubbling over with happiness, but, surprise, managed to hold sway over the size of our bouquets. Elizabeth had wanted large, flamboyant; Nancy, bless her, insisted on something a little more in keeping with my age and second marriages.

It's amazing how quickly Elizabeth set the ball rolling once the barriers were down. She suggested the beginning of the long school holidays for the ceremony so Graeme and I could go away for a few weeks. Their grandmother would stay with them and we'd be together for Christmas. It was a small wedding. Under the umbrella.

The Odd Salim Beg

Oh, glory, this is really it, Sarah thought. Is it the same, worse, better? Maybe I shouldn't have come at all after all these years.

It was a birthday present, her fortieth, from her parents and children, the fifteen year-old twins' contribution being their willingness to stay with their grandparents. She was tired; it was two in the morning at Delhi airport and already she didn't know how she was going to cope with the clamour.

'Please be moving along, madam,' sang the voice of the man behind her. 'Have you been to India before, madam? My countrymen they may be but they do take an interminable time to do anything, do you know. I am a businessman, do you know, and this is the very worst place for getting about in. You understand me?'

Sarah did, both his accent and his meaning, but was unable to get a word in.

'Here is my card, madam. Salim Beg. Importer and exporter. If I can be of any assistance, please to call me. Ah, here we go, a few more steps forward, isn't it. Oh, there you are, an opening there, isn't it. You can go to that officer. I am very pleased, madam, to be of assistance.' His rapid flow ended with a small bow as he manoeuvred Sarah towards the unoccupied Customs officer.

'Thanks. Thank you very much,' Sarah managed to reply, amazed at the man's volubility and her so quickly reaching this point.

With a bit of luck I'll be able to get a few hours sleep before the day starts, she thought. She had half-registered the up-to-the-minute decor, the smartness of the few armed guards dotted about, and the efficiency. Sixteen years ago it had been very different, untidy, officials being very officious, armed guards menacing. And her husband, suddenly seeing it as a visitor and not liking it. And then taking it out on her. Poor Raj, she thought, he should see it now. But he'd died when the children were five.

There were no auto-rickshaws, just black taxis lined up. She couldn't suppress a giggle; sixteen years ago, drivers of every form of vehicle would be fighting for their luggage, every driver cheaper than the other fellow, all with brothers or cousins who owned the very best hotel and knew the best places to shop.

And as she reached the top of the queue, Salim Beg appeared by her side. He waved his umbrella at the man opening taxi doors and installing passengers and luggage in appropriate places, saying, 'Madam, allow me to drop you off in my car. They are all thieves, isn't it, charging like the wounded buffalo, do you know,' and here a wheezy laugh emerged from his belly. 'Ah, here is my driver now, if you please.' He gave another little bow as he steered Sarah into his car and hopped in beside her. 'Now, Madam, where are you staying? I will presume to guess…you are at the YMCA.'

'Well, yes, as a matter of –'

'Oh very good, very clean, very central, do you know, and not too very expensive, isn't it. You have been to India before perhaps?' Salim Beg stopped speaking, stopped so absolutely Sarah had to look to make sure he was still there, still intact.

'Yes, I have been here before,' she replied slowly. 'About sixteen years ago. I was with my husband then.' She caught Salim Beg's raised eyebrow, his enquiring look. 'My husband died ten years ago.' Again she sensed his enquiry. 'No, I didn't marry again, I was busy working and bringing up my children.'

Salim Beg's silence now encouraged Sarah to tell her story, how her husband had ruined what should have been a wonderful holiday, getting to know his country, how his family had accepted but he seemed to reject her and how their marriage never went back to the way it had been before India. He had protected her from everything that was truly Indian, the ordinary people, the bazaars, street food. This time, she wanted to see everything, mix with everybody; catch the colour, the melody, that was India.

With a suddenness, the car stopped.

'Here we are, my very good and gracious madam. The YMCA. Please to call me if you need anything.'

As soon as she was out on the courtyard and the doorman had her bags, the car was gone. Goodness, it was as if he was never there, Sarah thought. Did I imagine it? If I did, am I imagining all this? But she was soon in a dreamless sleep between the crisp white sheets of the hostel.

Five days later, after a couple of tours of the city and her own private wanderings through Old Delhi, the spice market, some of the lovely buildings, she boarded a train for Jammu Tawi already knowing she would have to come back, bring the children. She also had the strange feeling of not being alone. She wasn't afraid but felt a presence, eyes upon her that were not wholly Indian. Oh well, she thought, whoever it is will surface at some time.

Caught up in the bustle of Jammu, finding the correct bus to Srinagar, Sarah again felt the force of someone's gaze. Turning suddenly, she sensed a movement as fast as a camera shutter but the scene was as she expected, dusty Indians going about their business. She boarded the bus with a feeling of excitement. Time, she thought, on the way back, to detour west to Amritsar, city of the Golden Temple, and east to Simla, where the British used to spend the summers in retreat from the inhospitable heat of Delhi.

Now, with the lulling motion and the velvety darkness, she thought of her first visit. She'd wondered if the tranquillity of the lake had veiled the passions of some who came here to spend time together on a houseboat; her vague jealousy of others' passions and now, why she thought it necessary to come back at all. Alone, she couldn't find what she didn't have before. But the feeling of those eyes reached her once again and with certainty she knew she was not alone. With that thought, Sarah gave herself up to the softness of the night.

With a sudden screech of tyres, shouts, bright lights and what sounded like gunfire, Sarah was alert. The bus had come to a halt and they were surrounded by an untidy lot of men who looked like army deserters, unshaven and belligerent.

The leader of the brigands boarded the bus. 'Not to be afraid, if you please,' he said. 'We are just wanting one of your number. Mr Salim Beg, will you kindly come out of whatever seat you have slid under like the slippery snake you are, and let these good people continue on their journey.' The dark eyes under the bright cloth wrapped around his head looked around the bus. They rested a moment on the startled face of Sarah.

The silent passivity of the passengers made it seem dreamlike. Sarah snatched a look around at her fellow travellers; she had not seen Salim Beg get on the bus, he had not approached her; it didn't seem like his kind of transport; again she had to doubt his existence.

At last there was a movement and a figure made its way to the front of the bus. It wasn't the Salim Beg she thought she knew. This one was in the Punjabi dress of *pugri*, the turban-like head covering with the end trailing down the back, long shirt over the many metres of fine cloth that go into the making of the salwar or trousers, these last two in white, and a waistcoat of bright silk brocade. It was completed with the toe-turned-up *gurgabi* on his feet. The contrast was so great, Sarah couldn't suppress a quick, nervous giggle while at the same time wondering just who this man was, why the brigands wanted him and why he had become involved with her holiday.

He gave Sarah an almost imperceptible nod as he passed and, as before, as soon as he alighted he, the leader, the rest of the gang, the lights, everything, just vanished into the night air.

This is ridiculous, Sarah thought as they were on their way again. I'm dreaming it; the man doesn't exist, he's a ghost, one of the Indian djinns, who just flits in and out of my imagination. The rest of the passengers, who appeared to all be Indian, had made no fuss, no protests; were now still minding their own business. She rummaged in her handbag to see if she could find the card Salim Beg had given her. Holding it in her hand, she thought, well, that's real enough, when she was suddenly startled by a person seating himself beside her. Hurriedly putting the card out of sight, her eyes turned to the stranger.

'It's all right,' he said, 'I have one too. Look.'

Her eyes went from the card in his hand to his piercingly blue eyes. The eyes Sarah immediately recognised as those she'd felt since boarding the train at Delhi. 'Why are you following me?' she demanded with a small shiver of fear in her belly. 'I'm here on holiday. My husband's family will secure the highest legal people if anything should happen to me.' With her faux bravado beginning to desert her, she said, 'Just tell me what is going on.'

'My name is David Cole and you are Sarah Ramraka. We will discuss these little events in Srinagar. You are quite safe. In the meantime, let us talk of other things.'

His manner was so relaxed it was almost reassuring but Sarah couldn't banish the fear she felt in the pit of her stomach. David talked; so many of his interests overlapped hers she couldn't help being drawn, reluctantly, into a kind of conversation. She did agree to have dinner with him on the large floating restaurant the following evening.

'Now just tell me what this is all about,' she demanded as soon as she was seated opposite David Cole.

'Ah, our Mr Beg is a man of many talents. We have known each other for many years. As I mentioned on the bus, in a roundabout way, I am a member of the British Diplomatic Corps. I spend a lot of time in the north of India. Some of Salim's activities teeter on the edge of legality but he does help an awful lot in one way or another. He's on to something now but last night's theatricals were most likely just that. Theatricals. And most likely to amuse you, Madam Ramraka. It means he likes you, approves of you.'

Sarah's eyes widened in disbelief, annoyance, but, if she let it, amusement too. She tried to hold onto annoyance. She wasn't there to be approved of, or not, by anyone and it seemed to her the very odd Mr

Salim Beg was getting the most amusement from his antics. She was, however, persuaded to spend more time with David, who could take her to places she would otherwise not have known about. And as he was seeing her off at Delhi airport for her return flight home, she agreed they should stay in touch.

Sometime later, it was in the safety of an Australian restaurant that David told her more of the story of Salim Beg. He said Salim had been trying to play Cupid for years. He'd thought it unnatural, immoral and a whole lot of other things that people should want to live alone. Not that David had wanted to, he said, it was just one of those things – the job, not meeting the right person and so on. Salim had told David to take that particular trip, saying it would be to his advantage. David assumed work, not romance. Salim had elicited enough information from Sarah in their very brief early meeting and his romantic little heart went to work.

The pair had of course seen Salim Beg more than once on that Kashmiri holiday and it would not surprise her at all if he popped up at the next table sometime, when she was enjoying a quiet morning coffee.

And had his connivings been successful? I leave that to your imagination.

The Teapot

The teapot had belonged to my aunt and from being a very small girl I had enjoyed our weekly afternoon teas. Aunt always treated me as a proper person; she didn't talk down to me and as a five-year-old I absorbed some of her olde worlde manners, most of which, I'm sure, have rubbed away in the busyness of living, and I appreciated the fine china teacups, the milk in pretty jugs. There would be cakes and tiny, crustless sandwiches on the three-tiered cake stand and at our weekly high teas, I was a lady. My aunt always appeared to match the fine floral patterns on the china with her own seeming fragility, her fine print dresses and pale pink lipstick.

My aunt used both hands to hold the teapot as she poured. As I grew older and bigger, aunt older and smaller, I took over the making and pouring of the beverage. I was always surprised by the weight of the pot and realised it was not only my aunt's fragility that had caused her to use both hands. It looked as if it should hold at least four cups but we were lucky to get just over two out of it, so I was forever topping it up. But we continued to use it because it was special, a part of our history. I thought it must have been a family heirloom with a longer history than mine and aunt's but she said she'd bought it just after the Second World War in a second-hand shop.

Auntie left me her fine china which unfortunately was used less often as life became busier. My friends and I used mugs and everything that would go into the dishwasher. I didn't have any nieces to whom to pass on the niceties of gracious living but I did eventually have a daughter for whom, I'm sorry to say, there was little time to spend on gracious living. I worked and she, from a very early age, was going to go out and conquer the world. She wasn't going to waste time on play-ing ladies. She did, however, present me with a granddaughter who was my aunt all over again. The fine china and the teapot again came into use. We had our weekly tête-à-têtes and once a month Amelia invited a friend to join us.

On one such occasion, our visitor's grandfather came to collect his granddaughter. He was invited to join the tail end of our tea party. I noticed his gaze kept returning to the teapot. I told him my short his-tory with it and he asked if he might hold it.

'Yes,' he murmured almost to himself, 'it is heavy.' He seemed upset.

I asked if something were wrong.

'I will tell you a story,' he said. He had once been a doctor, he began, and had had a very good friend who was a famous potter. They and many others with usable skills had been forced into working for their German occupiers, in their case in a factory making prostheses for in-jured German servicemen. Although their conditions of living were slightly better than that of their fellow Jews, the friends didn't envisage living a long and happy life. They had lost their homes and everything in them and neither knew the whereabouts or well-being of family members. Somehow, the friend had managed to hold onto, and hide, a teapot. Mr Gronski said how his friend had a fierce determination to leave behind some trace of his family.

He slowly told us that with the materials they had to use in their work, his friend painstakingly painted tiny portraits of his family on scraps of calico. It was very dangerous but he worked in the dead of night and Mr Gronski described he and others would act as lookouts for the surprise visits made by their guards. He painted his pictures with the limited colours available and took his teapot from its hiding place. The portraits were placed in its base and plaster placed over them, seal-ing it to the sides and smoothing it as much as possible. To harden the plaster, the teapot hung overnight just above the meagre fire they were allowed but which also kept their working materials in usable condition.

The teapot went back into its hiding place, Mr Gronski told us, but

his friend became more weak and ill until the guards took him away –
to hospital, they said, but Mr Gronski never saw him again.

The war was going badly for the Germans and suddenly the guards,
the administrators, vanished. For a whole day and night, there was
quiet. Even the prisoners spoke in whispers if they spoke at all. Then a
British battalion arrived.

'Well,' said our friend, 'eventually I find myself in this beautiful
country. But this teapot,' he said, tears now streaming down his face, 'I
think was my friend's. It is the design, you see, and here, on the bottom,
this sign…and the weight. It should not be so heavy.'

I asked Mr Gronski what he would like me to do and he, still holding on to the pot, could only say, over and over, 'Ah, my friend, and
many friends, gone, all gone.'

I told him I would take it to the Jewish Museum and if he would
like to come with me, he could tell the curator his story. They would
know what to do.

He put the teapot on the table but his hands stayed clasped around
it for some time. He seemed lost to us, his little audience of three.

The elderly man slowly came back to himself, and the place and the
time. 'Come, little one,' he said to his granddaughter, 'I must get you
home to your mama and papa. Forgive me,' he said to me, 'for my
lapse.'

We, Mr Gronski and I, did take the teapot to the museum and he
related his story. The staff said they would do what they could to check
it and they'd keep us informed.

Weeks and months passed but eventually a triumphant phone call
came to say the riddle was solved. The false base had been removed and,
indeed, five miniature paintings found. They were not in the best condition but also, on the inside base of the pot, had been written a story.
It must have been very difficult, they said, to print, in tiny letters, on
such a surface, but it gave names, dates, addresses. They had started a
trace on family members but did not hold much hope. They said I
could have my teapot back if I wished. I said I would ask Mr Gronski

if he would like it. The old gentleman said no, it should stay with the museum, a bit more of the story. So it, the delicate portraits and Mr Gronski's story are now behind glass. The words on the inside of the teapot are reprinted on card and beside the names et cetera are the most poignant words I think I shall ever read. They are, 'These are the things we do to keep our names in history.'

The historians who try to connect found objects with their original owners might one day be able to tell us how the teapot came to Australia but, for the moment, it is a mystery.

My granddaughter found another lovely teapot, unearthed in a dusty corner of a junk yard. It needed several years of dirt cleaning away but my granddaughter seemed to have been drawn to it and surprisingly, not a crack or a chip anywhere. It appears quite ordinary, not overweight, the maker's name is on the base but it pours beautifully and after many years of not being used, is again in service taking part in our afternoon teas. It, too, has a history, but one we shall certainly never know. My granddaughter and I make up stories about the people who might have used it and where they or their descendants are now.

The Diva

When she was three, she was a real little prima donna. All three-year-old baby fat, stamping her cherubic-like little feet, her dimpled hand on where her hips would be eventually, her chubby cheeks getting pinker as she demanded to know why she wasn't going to be the princess this time in the kindergarten concert. 'Because, darling, you were the princess last time and Linda wants a turn,' wasn't sufficient reason.

Joan's mother sided with the teacher but Joan's father believed when a star is born, it should take centre stage every time. Joan's father could see his little darling, in years to come, taking curtain calls without number, loved by everyone but belonging only to him. Naturally this caused tensions between the parents. Joan's mother was the one who took her to lessons, tried to instil reason, the idea of sharing, that someone else might be as good, or even better. It was Joan's mother who had to deal with the tantrums and appease the teachers, persuade them not to debar Joan from attending classes.

Of course, at home, Joan was Daddy's little girl and could do no wrong.

The ballet lessons continued; the succession of teachers unable to be either persuaded or bought, to unfairly favour Joan. In class, she was required to do the exercises like everyone else and when performances were scheduled, she'd have to accept whatever rôle assigned her. She was a member of a minor company in which she rather truculently accepted the position of understudy to the leading dancer. And that was only achieved by sweet talking and money on behalf of her father.

By now, Joan's mother had stopped driving her daughter to classes or rehearsals and didn't attend the performances. Within the house, she had become the almost silent figure who provided meals and kept the wheels turning. She herself attended evening classes and worked three days per week.

When Joan was sixteen, certainly not sweet and certainly not kissed in the sweet sixteen sense, she knew she was more than ready for the leading roles. She was having more tantrums and even her father had trouble keeping her happy. But as it happened, the company she was in was putting on a final performance. It was closing down due to financial reasons; even Joan's father, somewhat impoverished by the years of keeping his little Joan happy, and various teachers and company owner's palms greased, could not keep it going. And, as it happened, the leading lady had contracted the flu and couldn't dance.

Joan's father saw this as a great opportunity. The company's ending would be the great opportunity for Joan's beginning. He had posters printed, proclaiming his Joan as the next, the only, star of ballet, the phoenix rising from the soon-to-be-defunct little company. Here was the chance for bigger, better companies, to bid for this young star with years of money-spinning stardom ahead.

The new leading lady was determined to make people sit up and take notice. The finale had her take one last, flying leap from a rock, landing, her legs gracefully folded beneath her. In group rehearsal, she did, admittedly, achieve this perfectly. In private, however, she had inveigled one of the stage hands to raise the rock, little by little, until it was quite high and for the first time in her life Joan knew she really did have to practise if she was to perfect this very high leap.

On the evening of the single performance, Joan really felt ready. She'd sweet-talked the stagehand into raising the rock yet a few more centimetres and she could already feel the love, the adulation, of the albeit small audience. Never mind; it would be enough to send her on her way. Russia, Paris, everyone would want her.

Hours after the final curtain, Joan's father returned home. It felt unusually quiet, still. He turned on the light to see nothing but emptiness. Everything gone, no furniture, no paintings, just the old refrigerator with old food in it and two posters stuck on with magnets. One, the larger by at least four times, proclaiming the precious Joan as the new, big star of ballet. The other, somewhere between A4 and A5 in size, demurely announcing the operatic debut of Joan's mother in a local production. Across the larger poster were the words, 'I hope you and your little diva will be happy.'

The little diva lay in a hospital bed, paralysed. In raising the rock yet more, she had not considered the hanging props. She'd hit her head in jumping, causing her to lose balance and land awkwardly. She would never move again.

Joan's father slid to the floor, a crumpled mess.

Interrupted by Death

I was on my way to Kashmir. Not the best of times to be visiting but it had been arranged, it was business, my business, and I did hope to also revisit some of the old haunts. The political situation was delicate. Before Partition, all of this was India. Pakistan didn't exist and Kashmir was a state…well, it still is, but Pakistan is claiming it as theirs and Kashmir wants to be independent. I am part of a dying tribe and on a genealogical quest; I need to know the strength of my Namboordri heritage – prove, in fact, that I am a Namboordri descendant.

Brahmins are thought to be the top of the tree of the Indian castes but actually, the Namboordris were above them. Don't get me wrong, I don't want to toot my horn or lord it over anyone, I just need to know my history. And you know, the so-called caste system wasn't so entrenched before British colonisation. It suited them to divide us, set us against ourselves. And now, dammit, I'm more British than anything else. The Namboordris are fair, brown to black hair, green eyes, tall and slender. If I can prove my lineage, it would help in my negotiations with the crooks here.

Initially, I thought it would be difficult to hire a driver. Indians have a strong sense of survival, but Kapoor was more than willing. Mind you, it was going to cost me plenty. He had a good set of references and I had to believe he was as good a driver as he said. The mountain roads are still treacherous, always will be, I suppose, if only for the unpreventable landslides. And I may as well tell you, I was on a small mission for the Indian government as well. But that's just between you and me.

We were actually driving all the way from Delhi to Srinigar, a long way, and you ask, why not fly? It just did not suit my purpose. It meant overnight stops and I said I was a tourist, obviously with money enough, taking an easy sightseeing trip. Kapoor was a man of few words but I had enough to occupy me. Actually, I was a tourist, going to places I hadn't been before and I wanted to detour slightly and go to Dehra Dūn. That marks the end of the Northern rail line and my once-upon-a-time husband had spent a lot of time there. Yes, he was a civil engineer employed by the railways.

We were climbing all the time and while it was still warm in Jammu, we needed to get out some warm clothes because it would start to cool after that. There's nothing between Jammu and Srinigar, just narrow, winding, road. The views are spectacular and because of the climb and never knowing when one might meet a vehicle coming down, the going is slow. But as I said, there's a lot to see. It's like a little dance sometimes; you meet an oncoming vehicle, one of us has to back to the nearest spot wide enough to allow a passing. Sometimes your opposition just refuses to back even when you know you have to back for some distance to allow the oncoming driver room to continue. It has happened that we've ended up pushing two behind us back – it could be made to look very funny in a film, a bit hair-raising in real life.

We'd been driving along for some time with nothing happening when we came upon a car parked across the road which meant, of course, we had to stop. Kapoor told me to stay in the car; he wasn't getting out either but he did put his hand pistol by his side. Several minutes passed before one of the two men in the car got out and came towards us. I saw Kapoor's hand, his left, rest on the gun. The stranger didn't bend to speak through the window, which Kapoor had opened slightly, but put his fingers on the top and told Kapoor to open it further. Kapoor said that madam, me, would become cold. The stranger replied that madam should have thought of a hot-water bottle, and chuckled. Not necessarily a good sign, making a joke in this kind of situation, but he followed it with more of an order to lower the window.

I piped up then and asked what his business was with us. He told me it was with my driver, not with me. I asked why it wasn't possible to wait until we arrived in Srinagar and was told, ha ha, wasn't this the best office imaginable, this beautiful fresh air, the best views, the silence, ah, yes, the silence. And privacy, he added darkly.

He yanked open the door and pulled Kapoor out. Kapoor fired widely and his assailant knocked the gun from his hand, kicking it over the edge. Dangerous things, he said. He started speaking quickly and in low tones to Kapoor, forcing him to the boot of the car. I attempted to get out but by this time the other fellow was by the car training his gun on me. The first fellow raised his voice to tell me I had better stay where I was, his friend was a bit nervous. Kapoor was forced to open the boot and indicate his bag of belongings, which his assailant roughly grabbed with his free hand. He threw it to the chap guarding me, telling him something which was probably to check the contents, because that's what he was doing. He took out a package, seemed satisfied, kept it and threw the rest after Kapoor's gun.

Oh dear, said his captor, now you've no change of clothing. You'll get a bit smelly for madam and that won't do. You'd better go and get your belongings, whereupon he pushed him forcefully over the edge. The screams, I'll never forget. He turned to me saying, oh dear, you've lost your driver. Never mind, the keys are in the boot but leave them there for twenty minutes and then drive carefully on to your destination.

I did as I was told and on arrival in Srinagar went to the police station to relate the whole story, the British office, much reduced in staff, and the Indian government office, where I was at least listened to with what seemed some respect. But when I'd finished my tale, the officer said it was an interesting story but they had no record of a Kapoor driving me to Kashmir. He said they were expecting me, and had a note of the appointments I had made. He said he and his colleagues had thought I was being somewhat foolish in driving myself but that was my affair. I told him to check the State borders where we had to present ourselves and our ID. He said they would but what was the point? Madam arrived alone, was expected to be on her own, so nothing is amiss, is it, madam? Can you argue with Indian logic?

I never did find out what it was all about. My driver was obviously using the trip to carry out some business, legal or not, and for which side, I'll never know. Maybe in thirty or fifty years when official papers might be released, something of the incident might be mentioned, explained, but there's no guarantee of that, either.

My business there was quickly finished and I flew out, first to Delhi, where I needed to tidy up a few loose ends, and then south, to Kochi. I thought I'd visit Cape Cormorin before returning to the safety of London – although I don't think I'm ever going to feel wholly safe. I have had cause to look over my shoulder on occasion, check reflections in windows in case I'm being followed. Enough time has passed, I think, for me to be able to relax, and then someone bumps into me – well, the price to pay for the business I was in and, if I'm honest, one I wouldn't change.

Strawberry Fair

She'd told her, more than once, she'd gone above and beyond the call of duty. By the time she was ten, her daughter was telling her she didn't think mothering was a duty, more a matter of love.

Later, the daughter's psychology books described her mother as a 'zoo mother': keep the animals clean and fed, their enclosures clean and, in the case of humans, clothed. By the time the daughter had reached that stage, she'd been through the teen years of dating, exploring the cultural life of art, theatre, music, opera, for which she'd needed clothes. And this was where her mother excelled.

She didn't seem to think sitting up all night to finish making a dress was 'going above and beyond…' She didn't think she was encroaching, either, when she flirted with the daughter's boyfriends when they came home for dinner or just to pick her up. She'd spend hours going through fabric shops, choosing material she knew would suit her daughter. And it always did. There was only ever one piece the daughter said she didn't like, saying it looked like Regency wallpaper and her mother saying, trust me, you'll love it. And she did. It was made up into a shirt-waister, a shirt-style fitted bodice, slightly gathered three-quarter sleeves with a double cuff, fitted waist and a full knife-pleated skirt with two narrow bands of the fabric cut horizontally sewn around near the hem. It became one of the favourites.

It was obvious the mother enjoyed creating these beautiful clothes, from playsuits to pantsuits to ball gowns, and the daughter, can it be said, exploited her. She would take a bolt of fabric home, with a sketch of a dress she'd seen in a window perhaps, and expect her mother to make it for an occasion perhaps two days hence.

Years later, the daughter realised she'd been horrible; she also realised her mother had done the best she could. She hadn't known how to be a mother of a baby, infant, adolescent. She still wasn't mothering in the proper sense in making a slave of herself with her sewing, but it was something she could do, was good at, and she enjoyed creating something unique and lovely. And perhaps with the boyfriends, the daughter thought, she was living a delayed youth. The daughter would forever think of these years between twelve and her getting married as her couturière years. Events were remembered by what she wore. The all-time favourite was the strawberry frock.

None of it caused the daughter to love her mother or even like her, and there were other events that caused great pain. As a thirteen-year-old, she had a white, cotton piqué party dance dress. The fabric was printed with tiny strawberry clusters, three red fruit, a green leaf or two. It had a fitted bodice, cut straight across the top meeting sort of off-the-shoulder puffed sleeves. The gathered three-tiered skirt, ending below her knees, above her ankles, each frill separated with green binding; a green sash at the waist, long ties at the back. A bit Scarlet O'Hara-ish. She had a favourite beau and he and she and her dress, foxtrotted, waltzed, rock 'n' rolled many evenings away. She loved that strawberry frock.

She liked the sight of strawberries, heart-shaped, pulsating red. She had strawberries for breakfast, with peaches and cream; rich colours, rich taste. She'd think of them starting off as delicate white flowers, then red fruit beginning to form, growing bigger, stronger, redder, nestling on their straw beds, shaded by their beautiful deep green leaves. Back-aching picking, but fun if you're young or old and able. And they're so good for you, she'd muse, calcium, iron, though probably, drowned in a strawberry daiquiri, potent in other ways.

From an Israeli shop she'd bought a bowl, glass, very heavy, thick, rippled, dimpled, except for a smooth hem around the top. Everything looks lovely in it – a small salad, chopped fresh fruit, a trifle – but strawberries look especially inviting in it. Looking down into it, the shiny fruit matches the sun-caught reflections of the glass. Almost too good to eat.

She enjoyed looking out at Nature's creations, on land or sea, but never took to actually gardening. At one time, she thought she'd buy a strawberry pot – you know, one of those things with pockets around the sides. However, her friends told her they really weren't suitable for growing strawberries, so she never did. One of the gardens she owned had what she called a strawberry tree. It was a lovely old tree with fruit looking so like the berries she'd named it after. No one knew its real name or if the fruit was edible. Birds never ate it, so she just enjoyed looking at it.

Once, when she was little, her sister went to a fancy dress party as the Queen of Hearts. The one who made tarts. Of course hearts featured prominently: the bib of her apron, the pockets, and a row of them danced along the hem of it. She wore a crown encrusted with red heart-shaped stones. She carried a tray of real tarts. Strawberry jam, of course. The judge ate some and gave her first prize. Their mother had grown the strawberries, made jam and her own pastry: nicer than anything you could buy.

When her husband had ceased to be her husband, he'd sent an email one day. He said he had been thinking about her and the song 'that starts off 'Are you going to Strawberry Fair? had been running through his mind. He started to sing it out loud, he said, but he'd substituted the song's destination for the name of the place where she was living. He never bought her roses, strawberry's relations.

Horace Walpole lived at Strawberry Hill, a Gothic Revival home on the Thames in Twickenham. It's now part of the Greater London borough of Richmond and the house, which started life as a cottage in 1747, was transformed by Walpole into the mediaeval-style mansion, and which, in more modern times, became Saint Mary's Catholic Training College. It is quite likely that is where the Strawberry Fair was held. She loved the Thames and everything on and along it.

In the season, supper or dessert for friends would be dark chocolate biscuits with rich, red, juicy strawberries and cream.

She was telling me her story. I'd met her at an orchestral concert; we'd noticed each other at other events but at this, we were actually introduced. Over the ensuing months, I got to know her better; she had such an interesting life and one day I'd asked if I could write it. She was approaching eighty and had covered more than three-quarters of the twentieth century, itself one hundred years of notable events. But that day we'd had strawberries and cream after lunch.

I had to ask what had happened to the dancing beau.

For the first time since our friendship had begun, her face became hard, bitter, the only time I had seen her look old.

'He was my first love', she began. 'Perhaps he should have been my only one. He was two years older than I, been away from school for that time because he'd had polio. He was gentle, a good dancer. Better than I. It was accepted we were a couple, no one cut in. We didn't talk about our feelings, we didn't hold hands. The only time we touched was when dancing. But we knew.

'When he was sixteen he left school to take an apprenticeship; I stayed on to become an academic…yes, psychology, of all things. Why, do you think I was drawn to that? I was hurt he left and just dropped me; no phone calls, no letters, billets-doux. I couldn't understand it. And in those days, you must understand, girls didn't do the chasing.

'It was when my mother was dying and she'd read in the local paper my old school was soon to celebrate its centenary and former students were invited back. I noted the date and even booked myself into the evening dinner dance. I thought, I can always change my mind. She died, my mother, and some time later I went to the daytime gathering at my old school. I'd caught up with some of my classmates and then he came. The air was electric, the small group of friends simultaneously took a step back.

'It seemed my mother hadn't told me of the times he'd called in to my house on his way home from where he worked; I didn't ever receive the notes he'd left with her or the letters he'd sent. He was heartbroken when he was told I was no longer interested in him and he was not to call again.

'We danced that night and knew we'd missed out on something special. So strawberries are the only things now that connect him to me.'

Her face had relaxed again and she had a dreamy, faraway look in her eyes. Then it hardened and she almost spat out, 'Was that duty? Was that what she saw as her duty?'

All I could do was take her hand, tell her, just think of the strawberries.

Sali

There's this kid, Sali Dali, about fourteen or fifteen, who works at a market in Aden. He, his dad, older brother and cousins sell tent rugs. Sali is bright and enterprising; he manages to guide shore-leave visitors from the ships going through the Suez Canal and on to Mediterranean seas to the market and of course to his family's rug stall. It is only afterwards that the visitors, laden with rugs or clutching consignment notes and lighter in the hip pocket, realise how clever young Sali had been.

Aiden, Lacie and Diane Cadell are twenty-seven-year-old triplets, giving themselves a holiday after their parents' deaths and before opening a restaurant in the English capital city. Their father had been an archaeologist, spending much time at the digs of Egypt; their mother had been an artist, her subjects the people and buildings of North Africa and this area. They had died when a small plane they were in, crashed. Naturally, the children had had many holidays in and around the area. They weren't as naïve as many other travellers but they were beguiled by young Sali and ended by buying several rugs that would make great wall hangings in their new restaurant. Aiden and his sisters were actually staying in Aden for a few days; most of their travelling had been in Egypt, travelling down the Nile and revisiting several old digs. While in town, Sali was often in tow, pulling them towards his favourite shops and eating places.

At one of these eating places, Sali introduced them to Liaan and Dallia, two Sudanese girls who looked about twelve but were, in fact, closer to eighteen, nineteen. They were working at the café but it didn't look as if the owner gave them any of the food they served. They were actually runaways from their respective villages and marriages to old men they neither knew nor wanted. The owner of the café knew this and felt he could treat them as he liked. The girls certainly couldn't resort to the law and it was debatable whether they were better off or not. The Cadells were able to talk to Liaan and Dallia about some of the places they had visited with their parents and had some understanding of the kind of life the two girls would have been subject to.

Dallia and Liaan considered themselves lucky to have escaped their village, with life in Aden much better. Lacie, Diane and Aiden knew there was not much of a future for them and discussed the possibility of helping them get to England. By acting as sponsors and guaranteeing work for the two girls, they thought they had a good chance. When the idea was put to Dallia and Liaan, the two were overwhelmed by the kindness but didn't think they were sufficiently worthy or clever enough to work in the Cadells' restaurant.

However, the three siblings set the ball rolling for their repatriation through the office of the British High Commission, in the process making friends with Aled, one of the staff there. They had to return to London but asked Aled if he would keep an eye on the two girls in their absence. By this time, the owner of the eating house that employed them was taking more interest in them and Aiden asserted he could see the gleam in his eye and the metaphorical rubbing of hands while he thought of ways of exploiting the situation to his own advantage.

Aled had undertaken the difficult task of getting birth certificates or, if that was impossible, a précis of family history, and approximate ages, and he had made appointments for health checks. In London, together with getting their restaurant prepared for a grand opening, the Cadells had also put in motion the hiring of staff. The most they could do for Liaan and Dallia were temporary visas of two years. Lacie said they could deal with renewal, or whatever was to come, at a later date. Get them here first, she said, everything in its time. A chef and cooks had been employed and, more recently, the wait staff. They had a full complement and when Liaan and Dallia arrived, they would be extras. They would need training, acclimatisation, becoming familiar with London and English life.

And then Aled phoned. The girls had disappeared. He went on to recount events. He said initially their employer had insisted they just didn't turn up for work one day. He didn't know where they were, what had happened to them. And he was angry at the inconvenience caused and very hurt that after all his kindness to them…et cetera ad nauseam. When Aled reminded him it was in his house he kept them virtual prisoners, he changed his story to say the girls had escaped. Aled then asked him if his house was different from everyone else's in not having bars on the windows and doors being locked at all times. Aled said, with every question put, our greasy friend was sinking further into his own muck. And before too long, he asked his price. He said he would sell us the girls, one million pounds each.

The siblings gasped but Diane quickly said, 'He knows that's imposs-ible. He wants a Dutch auction until we reach a sum acceptable to all.'

All four said at once, 'But we don't do deals like that.'

However, no one wanted any harm to come to the girls. Had the Cadells not tried to help them, their lives would have gone on, they would probably be married, perhaps against their will but most likely to men a bit more acceptable than the old men chosen in their villages. The three Cadells felt responsible. They knew there were hundreds, thousands of young people, with potential, but because of their situ-ations it would never be realised. Too many would die early deaths, from disease, undernourishment, hard labour. They couldn't help them all; they had undertaken to help these two girls, had interfered in their lives, given them hope.

Aiden asked Aled if the embassy had a list of police who could be trusted. Yes, he said, but they were not likely to spend much time on a case like this. Too many young women disappeared and there were more important issues to be dealt with. What about enlisting Sali's help was the collective thought of the triplets? Aled had already thought of that and wanted to check it was okay.

'Well, I think it's our best bet,' Aiden said.

Sali continued to be the best guide of the area; his family continued to sell more rugs than any other rug-making family but he thought he might branch out a bit. He'd be treading on toes in taking visitors to areas of interest himself, so he persuaded tour operators to hire him. They all knew him, knew his persuasive ways, he already sent customers to them, customers who previously had no intention of taking trips to areas away from the safety of town.

They were happy to hire him more than just occasionally and of course, in this, Sali had more chance of picking up information. He was a natural in being able to ask the right, innocent, question, make a comment that elicited a stream of interesting chatter. Some of which contained the odd gem. Some about the girls and what was happening, although he hadn't found out their current location yet, but also some that was extremely useful to the embassy. Of course he didn't realise the value of what he passed on to Aled, just included it in his chatter. Aled did, though, and passed it on, up the line.

Several months had gone by; the Foreign Office wanted to know the status of the Cadells' sponsored guest, the new restaurant had opened and the three young restaurateurs were kept very busy. That didn't stop their pressure on Aled and, through him, Sali, to continue the search for Dallia and Liaan. Then at last, the call from Aled to say Sali had found them.

He saw them at a distance, so manoeuvring his little group of Americans closer and including the head of the village in his patter, with his eyes he indicated to Liaan that they were not to worry, help would be on the way. He knew they were still 'owned' by the café owner, knew they still had a price, which was why they were still unwed and not overworked. That is not to say they didn't have to 'earn their keep' and they were forced to work as prostitutes to select clients. Mr Café Owner was no fool. This did involve their trips over the border to Dubai and there was no timetable. Except, of course, once there, the stay was for several weeks. Visiting sheiks didn't make overnight stops. So the question now was, how to get the two girls out.

It was simple in the end. Jokingly, Aiden had said he and his boyfriend, George, could go in à la Lawrence of Arabia and somehow just spirit the girls out. He hadn't got so far as working it all out. As it happened, things were a bit quiet at the embassy and it was agreed that a party of 'officials' would go in, hire the girls and several hours later tell their captors their 'conversation had been very interesting'; they needed to take the girls to the embassy to 'interrogate' them. It was intimated they'd talked about illegal trade – smuggling, of girls as well as goods.

That is another story and one I am not privy to, but for the girls it was almost plain sailing. They arrived in London, were looked after, improved their English. In time, Dallia took over reception of the restaurant, took bookings and had a bit of Sali about her, a Pied Piper of customers. Liaan loved the kitchen, remembered and experimented with the recipes of her childhood and then taught the cooks. She needed help in writing them down and finding the English names of some of the ingredients. She would never marry, saying she could trust food and as far as she could see, it made everybody happy.

And Sali? Ah, yes, Sali. He couldn't have been more than nineteen when the Foreign Office employed him. He remained his own seemingly guileless self, and became more charming as he grew. He lived with his family, albeit with several trips away 'selling and delivering rugs'. When he was twenty-three or thereabouts, the family opened a shop in London because they really did make beautiful rugs, so it all fell into place. He was just as comfortable in a three-piece suit as in his loose pyjamas, loose pants and long shirt, and life went on. It took a while but he did, eventually, persuade Dallia to marry him.

With their combined Pied Piper qualities, there was no stopping them. A couple of years after their marriage, they opened a restaurant of their own on the edges of London. No doubt another, or more, would eventually open closer to the centre. Liaan stayed with the Cadells and took great care in keeping her recipes safe, not circulating amongst the cooking fraternity. Dallia tried all manner of tricks, coercion, to wheedle recipes out of her but Liaan's loyalty to the Cadells remained strong.

A Marriage

Can you tell us what happened, Mrs Castigan?

I killed him.

Who did you kill, Mrs Castigan?

My husband. I stabbed my husband and he's dead.

What did you use to stab him with? Can you remember? And can you tell us how you know you killed him? Did you see his body? Did you see any blood, Mrs Castigan?

Kitchen knife. He said I had. He said, 'You've killed me.' And I must have passed out then. I don't remember.

You've been very helpful, Mrs Castigan. The doctor is going to give you an injection now to help you sleep. Is that all right? We can talk again when you've rested.

Yes, so tired. Tired, I want to sleep. Call me Helen, please.

Mrs Helen Castigan was in her own bed and her daughter had agreed to stay with her. She wasn't under arrest but the police had said the usual things that included the instruction not to go anywhere.

Charles Castigan had phoned the police at three-fifteen that afternoon. He said his wife had tried to stab him, wanted to kill him. He said he was ringing from the garden; his wife was still inside the house. He thought his wife was insane; they had not had an argument and, no, she had not tried anything like this before.

At the house, in the kitchen, he volunteered the information he thought they were a happy couple, the occasional spat but what couple doesn't, eh? It was the second marriage for them both. They had worked overseas – yes, he was a civil engineer, his wife was actually a social worker. They had travelled, India a few times, the US a couple, Hong Kong, Singapore, Fiji, Canada… Yes, they had children from their previous marriages. He had no idea why she had suddenly gone off the rails and, no, he certainly would not press charges.

A few days later, a social worker, with a female police officer, was again questioning Helen Castigan.

Mrs Castigan, I'm pleased you're feeling better. Would you like to tell us how you see the events of the past few days.

Helen. Call me Helen, please. My daughter said he's left the house.

She was told that was correct. He was staying with his elder son. And yes, he was very alive and well.

Helen let out a long breath and visibly calmed.

It goes back a good while before a few days ago…

Let's just start there, shall we?

Well, it's his silence, it went on for longer this time. More than silence, it's as if I'm not there, I become invisible, a non-person. Not a word, nothing. He even sleeps in the same bed, our bed, but nothing. If I try to touch him, he freezes more. No goodnight, no good morning, not even pass the salt please and I used to say that was about the limit of conversation in my first marriage. She gave a grim chuckle; I thought I'd married a man with intellect, knowledge, a conversationalist… Well, I did. He just switches it off sometimes.

Tell us about the ice, Helen. What's that about, what's it like?

It's like he's built an ice wall around himself. It's cold, he emanates cold, like walking through the cold section of the supermarket. He seems as trapped in it as much as I'm locked out. And this time, after a month, after I've pleaded, shouted, tried to guess, whatever it was that I did to upset him…because that's what happens – he takes offence at something and withdraws, builds this wall. Then finally he'll say, well, on such and such a day, at a precise time, like two thirty-seven and fifteen seconds in the afternoon, you said, did, whatever sin I'd allegedly committed. And I can't remember such an event. I mean, it's not an event, and so trivial, infinitesimal. But I do say, ask him, why he didn't mention it at the time. The thing is, at the time he would have not have considered whatever I said, did, served, as important either. But something percolates and, well, that's what happens.

Helen, you said this behaviour has been happening for some time. Can you tell us when it started?

Yes, it's hard to say, really. Everything seemed okay for the three years before we married. Well,, sort of, I suppose… He quit his job – he always felt discriminated against. He really is a good engineer, he's done some brilliant work but never could get to the top echelons in the scheme of things. He has a psychology degree as well and when he had to decide what branch of psych he'd take, he decided against counselling, took organisational – he's used that in his engineering work. I said at the time, good choice 'cause you're not a people person. Yes, thank you, a cup of tea would be lovely.

So Helen, early on in your relationship you realised his personal skills were…well, not suitable to equip him as a clinical psychologist? What happened when he quit his job?

No, yes, they weren't. He did volunteer work for meditation people. He was back and forth to a job they were doing in the Blue Mountains. Building a big centre or something. As far as I know, it was never finished. Like many of the movements' projects. He was in charge of a project in Cambodia at one time, building a university. I don't know what happened to that. But anyway, it seemed we were on again, off again, with our relationship. I wanted something more permanent, at least steady, to know where I stood. I said to him, he had to make up his mind, marry me and settle down, get a job and so on or we were finished. I needed to move on. Well, he married me.

Shall we take a break, Helen?

Yes, please.

He belittled me – all the time. In private, we discussed things, topical, controversial – we're both philosophers, too, and sometimes our thinking veers away from the popular view. Then, at a party or a dinner, with other people, that topic might come up. I would give my views, thinking he would back me up but instead he'd tell me I was stupid for thinking that way. He is, was, so clever at twisting things. He would get the others to laugh at me. It was no good trying to discuss it afterwards. I was beginning to doubt my sanity. And then, now, I guess I just couldn't cope any more. I had to crack the ice. I don't really remember but the knife would have been on the bench top and I stabbed him. I really thought it would hit ice. I am mad – he's right. Do his children know I killed him? My children, have they been called? Oh, of course; Susie's in the kitchen. I'm so sorry.

You didn't kill your husband, Helen. There's not a drop of blood on the knife or anywhere else. Certainly not on your husband, who is very alive and well.

Helen might have been pleased to hear that, been reminded it was true, but at the same time she shrank into herself, as if she were trying to get away from something that frightened her.

Why did he tell me I'd killed him?

I don't know why he did that, Helen.

Helen stayed in the psychiatric ward of the local hospital for the next few days, protected, resting, talking. The social worker visited several times.

About a week and a half later, she visited and said, We have discussed your case, Helen. No damage has been done and your husband isn't pressing charges for anything. There's nothing, really, to press charges on and the psychiatrist feels you're well enough to leave. He would like you to keep on seeing him and I also recommend that you do, but that's up to you. But now, I want to talk to you about where you'll live. You have grounds on which to divorce your husband, mental cruelty, if you want to go down that path. He's been having meetings with a different psychiatrist. It has been recommended he maintain those and I understand if he doesn't do that voluntarily, a judge will give an order to make them compulsory. We've met both sets of children, several times, separately and together. Your stepchildren would like to see you – they're very fond of you, it seems. Your elder daughter said she would like you to stay with her, at least for the time being, but you can discuss that with her. But we gained a deeper insight into the behaviour of your husband. They didn't have an easy life, it seems.

The marriage had ended already but eventually the formalities were dealt with and Helen became free. Her stepchildren were able to report on their father, who, it turned out, was found to be somewhere on the autism spectrum. Helen, with all her training, couldn't believe she didn't see it herself. Too close, she said, and she wanted to believe in her husband. Wanted what she saw in him in the beginning. But how easy it is to manipulate the mind.

Happy Birthday

He was at his parents' house polishing his old and precious Morgan. There was not a lot to polish – a two-seater sports car with fold-back hood. The leather seats and generous pockets on the insides of the doors had to be kept supple, though, and although the hood was mostly up, being folded only for its weekly spin, weather permitting, it had to be maintained. It lived here, at his parents' house, because his own inner-city two-up, two-down didn't boast a garage and it wouldn't have lasted very long on the street.

Even working on the car, he exuded an air of wealth. No chain store shorts or shirts for him and only top brand name sneakers on his feet. The car, the clothes, were an accepted fact of his style. He could buy what he wanted and his manner was easy charm, complementing his dark good looks and medium height. His body was perfectly proportioned with shiny black hair, which, if he let it grow a bit, as now, curled around his ears. His eyes were dark brown but not so dark as to be un-fathomable. Today they looked troubled.

'Well, Ramesh, thirty today. Nice round figure, eh. Not too old, not too young.'

'Oh, hi, Dad. Yes, I suppose thirty sounds pretty sensible.'

'Time to think about settling down, don't you think?' continued Satish.

Ramesh took some time before replying, continuing to make slow circles with the polishing cloth on the already-gleaming long, British green bonnet. He thought of his friends, some married, by arrangement through the manipulations of the respective parents, others engaged and all to other Indians. He thought of Hema and the very few times they'd been out together, always in a foursome, or more, and always home at a reasonable time. Her father always waited up and saw there was no lingering between car and front door. She was a nice enough girl, Ramesh thought, but he wasn't exactly champing at the bit to settle down with her. As far as he could see, they didn't really have a lot to talk about.

'Well,' he said at length, 'you've been thinking about it for some time, haven't you? How many meetings have you arranged so far? Ten? Fifteen? All nice girls with the right family backgrounds. Sorry, Dad, I don't mean to sound cynical and I know I agreed to doing it this way but somehow I just don't feel ready or something. Perhaps,' he ended lamely, 'I haven't found the right girl yet.'

Humpf, he thought to himself, it's not that I'm not ready, I'm more than ready. How many other thirty-year-old fellows in this country, this country that I was born in, would have had no sexual experience at all except for a brief fling at uni. with one girl? The guys at work would laugh if they thought a fellow would, could, 'save himself' for marriage. Trouble is, I don't know who I am.

'Well, don't forget,' Satish interrupted his thoughts, 'Hema and her parents will be here for your birthday dinner tonight. This is the third time we've had them over and Hema's father will be expecting your signature on the dotted line. Oh, don't look so startled,' he chuckled, 'marriage isn't that bad. In fact, it can be quite good for you and you don't want to turn into a crusty old bachelor, do you?' He turned to go. 'See you upstairs after you've taken the car out for an airing?'

'Yes, Dad, of course,' and Ramesh slipped into the comfortable leather of the driver's seat, his right forefinger idly tracing the steering wheel, seeing nothing. The image of the card he'd received yesterday came into his mind. 'Love from Mum', it said. The mother he denied. She'd said once she'd sign her name Catherine, if it made him feel any better, but he hadn't been able to come to terms with that either.

Why had she left him? She'd said he couldn't deny his English side any more than he could claim to be totally Indian. But she had denied him, so he could deny her and everything to do with her, including her Englishness. He thought he had it all in proper perspective and was getting on with his life quite nicely, thank you very much. In his mid-twenties, he'd even been able to communicate with her and see her when he went to Melbourne on business for his law firm. Then there'd been no contact for a couple of years since that trip when he'd bumped into a colleague and introductions became necessary. Later, they'd had a heated argument over it. She said he couldn't dismiss her as 'just a person I know here' and he said she had no right in saying 'but I'm your mother'.

Everyone who knew him accepted his stepmother as his mother even if they dimly remembered the real one; the biological one. Kamala had been there since he was eleven, after all, was Indian, like his dad, and there was no denying they had provided him with a comfortable life and education. Their friends had become almost totally Indian and it was more comfortable not to think of the 'Anglo taint'.

After that incident with his mother, he said he'd now have to explain things to his colleagues and it would be embarrassing. His mother had said that three-quarters of today's youth lived with a parent not their own. No big deal. No stigma attached to that, she said. But was it that, or the fact that she walked out on him and his father, and his young brother? If he admitted to two mothers, he might have to explain why she left. If he thought about it, would he find just cause? If he found just cause, then his father was, to some degree, at fault. Just as well I'm not in family law, he thought wryly. And no, my father's perfect and she's wrong, all wrong.

Even this car – he knew his mother would have given it to him after the death of his grandfather, the man he hadn't met again after his mother left. But he wouldn't accept anything from her and when he saw it advertised for sale, as he knew it would be, he negotiated for its purchase through a colleague. It had nothing to do with its being a family relic, everything to do with his interest in classic cars. Since being very young, Ramesh had a passion for collecting models of them. He didn't know if his brother had ever told their mother about the purchase; it never came up in conversation and some part of him told him not to think about it.

He'd wanted to identify as Indian. Do everything the Indian way, including having his wife chosen for him and remaining chaste until then. It wasn't that he wasn't popular; he was. He could chat up girls better than most fellows he knew. He'd taken plenty out but it never went beyond the casual and he never allowed his physical needs to rule him. Flashes of what was his regular life went through his mind; it was the girls who came to ask him to dance at nightclubs, girls who came to sit next to him at bars. Female glances at restaurants, all in his direction. His friends said it wasn't fair. One or two of the married fellows had kept on seeing their particular Anglo-Australian girlfriends and several of the engaged ones carried on with double lives. All shits, he thought, bloody hypocrites. He wasn't interested; maybe that was the attraction.

There'd been that girl at uni, Rebecca, with her bouncy black curls and bouncy personality. She'd been a wiz at languages, he remembered, and now, he knew, she was in international law. If he could feel about someone else the way he'd felt about her, then he'd know it was right. During their last summer break, they'd had a brief holiday in India and they'd visited the small Jewish sector in the south. That was when the argument blew up and she'd accused him of not having a mind of his own, doing 'what Daddy wanted' she taunted. Wonder where she is now? Did you ever get a second chance?

He felt sick, inadequate. Could he love someone because she was his father's choice? He'd have to produce his birth certificate for the marriage licence. His mother's name was on it. A wife would want to know about her, perhaps to meet her, women being what they are. If there were children, would they want to know their 'real' grandmother as well?

He thought of the friends his father and mother had had before the separation. They seemed to have just faded out of their lives after she had gone. He had trouble recalling their images but they were such a cosmopolitan lot: such crazy mixtures of Chinese with Italian, White Russian and Indian – they were nice, wonder what happened to them. There was that really dark, tall fellow from Kenya married to an Englishwoman. But all now, or then even, Australian citizens. They're probably all still here in Sydney somewhere; wonder if they're still in touch with Mum. The Chinese woman, now he thought about it, was from New Zealand but her mother didn't speak English and their little boy, five or six years younger than himself, spoke Chinese to his grandmother, Italian to his father's aunt and English to everyone else. Clever little kid. He still struggled sometimes with his Hindi, not having started to learn the language until his father married his stepmum.

No, Ramesh thought, pulling himself out of his reverie, I think I'll have to stay single. It's all too difficult to think about. Won't please Mum and Dad but I'll tell them now, no to Hema and no more introductions. He eased himself from behind the steering wheel and gently closed the door. Leaning into the car, his head resting on his arms, a huge wave of sadness swept over him. I feel as if I'm losing everything, he thought, I don't even want the car, and he splayed his fingers over the roof even as the rest of him gathered itself together for the walk upstairs.

'Hey, son, you haven't taken the car out for a spin yet. Better get a move on, eh?'

'What? Oh, yes, sorry, Dad, I'm not going to accept Hema and I don't want any more introductions and I don't think I'll be here for dinner tonight,' he said, in a rush.

'What do you mean, you won't be here for dinner? Your mother's gone to so much trouble, it's your birthday, what do you mean "no to Hema"? What's the matter with you? This is the third family visit. You've been taking her out. It's expected, you know that. They'll be arranging her trousseau and their guest list. They'll have talked to their friends. Oh, it's just cold feet. Here, have a drink, sit down, let's talk about it.' And Satish poured another whiskey, took his own and Ramesh's and steered his son to the sofa.

'Here,' he said, handing Ramesh the glass, 'drink this. Come on, it's your birthday. You're thirty, doing well, have everything you need, or want, except a good wife and soon the patter of tiny feet, eh,' he finished, with a gentle punch to Ramesh's arm, and a slightly hollow laugh.

'Is that the way it's supposed to happen, Dad? Man has stable job, gets wife, has baby, cements the marriage and if it's a boy, secures the family line, and if it's a girl, another baby next year. Is that it?'

'Is that what?' asked a feminine voice as Kamala, Satish's wife, came into the room. 'Bit early for whiskey, isn't it, even if it is a birthday and important decisions to be made, eh?' She finished with a merry little laugh and a light pat on Ramesh's shoulder.

'Go away, Kamala. This is men's business. Go and get us something to eat,' ordered Satish.

Ramesh quickly looked up and caught the hurt, squashed look on Kamala's face as she turned to do as she was bid. 'No,' he said, 'don't go. I'd rather this was family business. It's just that I've told Dad I don't want to marry Hema,' Kamala took a loud intake of breath and put her hand out to the back of the sofa, 'and at this moment, don't want to marry anyone. And I'm sorry, Mum,' he said, looking up at her, 'I won't be here for dinner.'

He put his untouched drink on the coffee table and stood up. 'I'm sorry, really sorry. Things shouldn't have gone as far as they have. I just didn't know – I have to find myself, know who I am, before I can... settle with anyone else. I'm going home. If I can do anything...' he raised his hands beseechingly before finding his way to the stairs and soon there was the grumble of his motorbike, his everyday transportation, fading into the distance.

'Oh, the stupid boy,' Satish snapped, roughly putting his own glass down after gulping the contents. 'I'm sure it's just a hiccup but if he's really not going to be here, I'll have to make excuses to the Mehras. Has he said anything to you about this? Arun might know something,' and he made his way to the telephone thinking tummy bug, early birthday celebrations with the boys, et cetera.

Arun, the younger son, knew nothing about his brother's plans or state of mind but suggested his father try to ring him, elicit more information before talking to the Mehras. This he tried to do but simply got the answering machine on the home number and 'out of range' for his mobile. Satish said he'd go to his home office to try to make some excuses for the possibility of Ramesh's non-attendance and the delay in announcing an engagement due, he was sure, to some minor difficulties. He told Kamala to ring everyone else, cancelling the evening.

The first call Kamala made was to Arun. They didn't see so much of him; he was what you'd call 'his own man'. He was respectful to his father and stepmother, who had had more influence in his life, coming into it at an earlier age, but Arun still went his own way. He was living with an Australian girl, had disregarded the Hindu dietary laws since the age of eight, asking his father what he was supposed to tell his friends when he went to their family barbecues, telling him Catholics no longer ate only fish on Fridays, so work it out. Yes, he had Indian friends, liked Indian food, music, even some of the customs, but he regarded himself as totally cosmopolitan or, if he wanted to be rude, a mongrel. And he didn't feel guilty if he occasionally phoned his birth mother, whom he easily called Mum. In his student days, she'd even been to visit, staying in his shared house. Admittedly it hadn't gone so well, inviting her to join a house of rowdy young males whom she didn't know at all and the two of them who really only knew who the other was without that real knowledge of each other, was an invitation for disaster. But he'd tried and they didn't talk about it. Sort of like a bad dream on the edges of consciousness, and the three or four phone calls a year continued. Satish and Kamala knew, he made no secret of it; they just didn't discuss it.

'Arun, it's Mum,' Kamala said into the phone.

'Oh, hi, Mum. What's this about Ramesh? Dad sounded like he was in a bit of a flap. Ramesh done a runner or something?'

'He says he's not coming tonight, says he won't marry Hema. Do you know what's going on?'

'No, I don't know anything. He doesn't exactly confide in me, you know. But I suppose it's better to find out before you get to the altar rather than after it, in a manner of speaking. Anyway, I haven't seen him for ages. Must be seven or eight weeks since Caro and I met him at Darling Harbour for a drink. He was with Mohan and Venu. He seemed okay. Chatted for a while and then Caro and I went to the pictures and they went off to do whatever they had planned. Shall I go round and see him? Is he at home?'

'Oh, Arun, thank you,' sighed Kamala. 'Yes, he said he was going home but he's not answering the phone and must have turned off his mobile. Just see if it's cold feet only. Your father is in a rage in the study, trying to make some excuses to the Mehras. He says I've got to ring everybody and tell them not to come and I don't know what to tell them and I've got all this food prepared. What shall I do with it, do you think?'

'Look, Mum, if Ramesh is serious about this, the word's going to get out pretty quickly. Don't ring anyone else, let them come, and Dad can make an announcement or whatever, tell them what he likes. Bit of a wake without a body. Sorry, not funny. I'll ring Dad on the office line and persuade him and then I'll go and see Ramesh. And how about if Caro and I come a bit early tonight, give you a hand? How does that sound? Okay, see you soon.'

Ramesh opened the door in response to the knocking. Without a word, he turned and walked back into the lounge and back into the chair he'd just vacated. Closing the door behind him, Arun followed but continued into the kitchen, where he started boiling water and putting coffee into two mugs. He carried the drinks back to the lounge and, placing one in front of Ramesh said, 'Want to talk about it?'

'What is there to say?' Ramesh replied, drawing the hot coffee mug into his two hands. 'I just don't know who I am any more. I don't know where I'm going and I sure as hell don't know how to get there. I know I've made a mess of things. Dad'll be as embarrassed as hell, Hema will lose face and I don't know what her chances of other "offers" are, but I just know I can't do it.'

'Well, it's not the end of the world,' replied Arun wryly, 'but you are going to be the talk of the town for a while. And, you realise, your name is going to be mud with all the Indian matrons for quite some time to come. Perhaps you could leave the country – no, no, joke. Sorry, not funny. Second time I've said that in the last couple of hours.'

'When was the first time?'

'I told Mum not to cancel any more guests for tonight. They're all going to find out sooner or later. May as well face the throng en masse. Yeah, I said it'd be a wake without the body. Unless, that is, you want to come and do the right thing and face them yourself. Dad rang Mr Mehra, Mum said, but didn't elaborate. However, I take it they won't be there for dinner. Dad'll probably see Mr Mehra in his office "at his earliest convenience". All very businesslike.'

'It is businesslike, isn't it? I thought, what difference does it make who I marry? You can love almost anyone if you put your mind to it and choosing someone like that means they've checked that our temperaments match or complement, or whatever they're supposed to do. Our aspirations should be similar but I've never heard her express an opinion on anything. Not surprising, I suppose, since I've never seen her alone. Everything she says or doesn't say comes from her father or mother. We're both healthy. It's a wonder they haven't counted our teeth, and we'll have beautiful, healthy children and she'll cook the kind of dishes I like, pamper to my needs and generally won't interfere with my life. Just like Mum. You know, she came out of the kitchen and said something and Dad ordered – ordered – her to go back there. I told her to stay. It was the first time I saw what a little life she has.'

'Mm,' came from Arun, sprawled opposite, coffee half drunk, legs outstretched, head resting on the back of the armchair.

'She's worked all her life, hasn't she? Part-time since she married Dad, but she took us on. That couldn't have been easy. I wonder why they didn't have a child of their own. And she runs the house like a bloody hotel without the staff. There's always people to dinner, relatives come to visit. She even acts as a tour guide for them in between everything else. I've never properly seen it; never thought about it, just took and took. And I'll end up just like Dad.'

'Mm,' murmured Arun during the pause.

'Will you stop just bloody saying "mm",' shouted Ramesh as he slammed his coffee mug on the table.

'What would you have me say, older brother? A few of the scales seem to have fallen from your eyes, I'm sorry you're in a mess, but glad, too, in a way. At least you're thinking. What about tonight – how about facing the party yourself? I think it would help Mum in some way. I spoke to Dad and he grudgingly agreed that addressing the crowd might be better than news just drifting out. At least they'll get our side of the story first. And some people will support you, and others will think you're just shit, but hey, what are friends for? Seriously, Ramesh, I think you should be there. You started the ball rolling and you can't walk away from it just like that.' He was leaning towards Ramesh, cradling his coffee mug, arms resting on his knees. 'Caro and I will be there and we'll support you. You know, surprising as it might sound, Caroline actually likes you.'

Ramesh looked up from the patch of carpet that should have been burning from the intensity of his non-seeing gaze. 'Does she?'

'Yes, of course she does. You can't see past her pale Anglo-Saxon face that goes against what you think you should believe in. She says you're clever, have a great sense of humour when you let it out, definitely rich – and, if I'm not careful, she'll leave me for you and live in luxury for the rest of her life. However, you'll have to kill me first. And she does wish that you would remember, at least sometimes, that the same Anglo-Saxon blood that's in her is also in us. Well, not the same or we'd be genetically unsuitable and all blood's red, anyway, but you get the drift. We have a biological mother from a world you've so far refused to inhabit. You've cocooned yourself in a culture miles away from its source and it's probably changing there just as quickly as life everywhere else.'

'My God, you go on. Have, have you spoken to her lately?'

'Couple of days ago. She asked about you, as she always does. Told her there'd be wedding bells, or the Indian version thereof, pretty soon. She wished you well. Look, Ramesh,' Arun continued, to his brother's startled look, 'the third visit from a girl and her family is almost the same as reading out the banns. Even I know that. You've let it go on and on. You've met with Mr and Mrs Mehra on several occasions, you've been going out with Hema, they've accepted you as part of the family. What did you think was happening?'

'I really have made a mess, haven't I? I should phone the Mehras, apologise or something. That's the least I can do. Hang about, I might need you. And how did you know, anyway, how many times I've met with the Mehras?' asked Ramesh as he started to get up.

'No,' said Arun, 'don't ring yet. Give them a couple of days. Right now, Hema will be having hysterics, Mrs Mehra will be pulling her hair out while trying to calm both husband and daughter, all the while thinking of the smirks on the faces of their friends as they pretend to console her by telling her what a bastard you are. And Mr Mehra will be furious. I think you should arrange to meet him in his office and try to talk it out, man to man.'

'You seem to know a lot about it, considering, as you say, you're not part of the cocooned set.'

'I might not be as immersed as you are but I am, don't forget, half-Indian, with parents who live a totally Indian life and one which I grew up in from the age of eight. If anything, I should be more Indian than you, as it got me at an earlier age. However,' Arun continued, 'I probably see more from the sidelines and you forget, Mr Mehra and I work at the same university. Might be different faculties and top and bottom of the hierarchical scale, but we Indians have to stick together, isn't that so?' Arun assumed the head-shaking sing-song actions so depicted of Indians. 'He seeks me out in the canteen and tries to steer me towards a "good Indian wife" while dismissing my current arrangement as a youthful aberration. I think I was an embarrassment, a bit of a blob, on this otherwise perfect arrangement for his daughter. Now, of course,

I shall get the blame. A bad influence – and I'm only the younger brother. Ah, well, we all have a cross to bear,' he said mischievously. 'How about tonight? Think you can make it over, face the crowd? You only have to do it once and then you can keep to yourself or whatever,' he finished, more seriously.

'Sorry, I didn't realise you'd be so involved as well. Just never thought. I mean, I never knew anyone from the other faculties, didn't join anything, just studied. Even now, all my friends are in the legal business. You lecture in philosophy and English and play in a jazz band in your spare time. So are Dad's, if you think about it. In the same business as him, I mean. Does Mum have friends of her own, do you think? Talk about her small life, mine's no better.'

'I wouldn't think Mum had much time for separate friends but don't be too hard on yourself. There's hope yet. What about tonight, then? Do you want Caro and me to pick you up?' suggested Arun.

'Yes, I'll be there. Might not be pleasant but I'll have to face the music at some time. Dad'll be mad as a hornet but I should get his sting directed at me and not at Mum, she being on hand. Not her fault. But I'll make my own way there, that way I can get away when I want or need. Will you tell them? Please?'

'Yeah, I'll go back that way. Don't think about it too much, eh, brother. It will sort itself out in time. See ya, okay?' and Arun let himself out of the house and back to his old, battered blue Mazda. Strange world, he thought, but who'd have it any different. Caro will be…what? Not pleased – optimistic.

Reminisce

I pass a house, with a steep-gabled roof, a shuttered attic window, dormers at the back. The first-floor bedrooms have Juliet balconies. Every time I see the house I think of snow, my childhood and snowmen. It's a house where children might visit but it looks like a grandma and grandpa kind of place, neat, and very quiet.

The contents of the attic – I imagine a doll's house, a trunk of dress-up items, Paddington Bear badly in need of a new coat and Pooh's fur patchy and thin. I hear Paddington telling Pooh about the joys of travel and how much he misses Peru while Pooh mourns the lack of honey. I think of the people who built this house, with a roof designed for snow to slide off and land with a thunk, so that someone has to clear the front path. But the very location of this house, in subtropical Queensland, makes it a fairy tale place, forever wreathed in climbing roses and green shady trees, at most getting a drenching of rain.

Do the owners, I wonder, get Christmas cards from far away, cards with pictures of snow and do they miss a place where once they lived? A place where the Christmas puddings would have been hanging in the cold pantry since late October early November, and the children have already taken their turn at stirring the Christmas cake and made a wish. It's a tiny house, really, a cottage, a memory transplanted. It reminds me of my first impressions of Launceston, Tasmania. I'd arrived in winter; snow covered the tops of the hills and the winds blowing down from them were cold. The architecture and layout of the city was reminiscent of a small patch of old London, miniaturised; a bit like a market town into which a few wealthier squires had decided to set up house. The city workers wore black and my abiding memory is of men in tight-fitting suits, bent into the wind, rubbing warmth into cold, ungloved hands – Dickens's character Uriah Heep, to a T. Mozart and his contemporaries would have felt quite at home in Launceston's theatre.

Those early white settlers who built the city certainly wanted – needed, perhaps – to transplant what they knew of their old homes now on the other side of the planet. Can any of us who move vast distances to resettle, ever, entirely, leave that first home behind? We might not build a replica of the house we remember but what tokens of memory might be inside the home? Do the stories of one place intermingle with those of the new place and thus create a bigger history?

I feel a lightness of heart, passing that house. Of course the balconies remind me of Romeo and Juliet, which, while not a happy story, does make one think of true love, of music and dance. The two ballets that remain strong in my mind are *Swan Lake*, seen in London when I was five, and my grandmother had taken me down to the capital not long after the end of the second world war, but the other was *Romeo and Juliet* performed by the Queensland Ballet Company in the 1990s. I imagine dancers on the lawns under the balconies but perhaps with a bit of the flavour of *West Side Story* thrown in.

Of course I do not stop to look at the house; I take in what I can while I pass. I want to see a swing fixed to a tree in the back garden and hear the ghost of laughter as it gently moves in the breeze. It was not my house, the house I pass, though it reminds me of the one that was, a very long time ago.

The Bicycle

My intention had been to arrive in Launceston, where I had never been before and knew no one, buy a nice little house and live happily ever after. Fairy stories, children, rarely come true. I could not find the nice little house, at least I couldn't find the one that said to me, 'I am yours' and that was the beginning of the story. The last remaining agent who hadn't ditched me as being impossible to please was beginning to despair. He had one last house on his books that I had not yet seen. He said it was not worth looking at but, 'Come on', he said, 'let's give it a go.'

We pulled up at a house that had definitely seen better days and was, actually, not safe to live in. As my first foot ventured to the footpath, I read the badly handmade tin sign, hammered into a veranda post, roughly painted white with black lettering proclaiming 'Tresparssers will be Persecutted'.

I tried to hide my smile. I couldn't stop the words tumbling out, 'I love it.' I did a pirouette in the dark, filthy hallway and again said I loved it. It was a hundred years old, with high ceilings, fireplaces in every room, timber floorboards six inches wide. I could see its possibilities and it was shouting at me, 'I'm yours, I'm yours.' I bought it.

I had found lovely lodgings in a B&B in which I had a bedsit with kitchen facilities sufficient for my needs. I had negotiated with the managers, explaining I wanted something comfortable as I looked for my dream home. It was on the edge of town, while my new house was a little further out, on the other side of town but still just a walk away. I continued in my bedsit while work was done on the house. As I said, I had known no one in Tasmania but I was so lucky with my choice of workers; artisans, every one. The head man, a master builder, with his wife and sister, became my friends.

Slowly but steadily, the house was coming back to life. I brought it into the twenty-first century but kept its historic features. It had central heating put in, but the beautiful fireplaces remained. The old claw-foot bath was fully renovated, the bathroom made slightly bigger – it was already big – and a separate large quarter-circle shower installed and all the plumbing replaced. Floors had to be replaced in some rooms and there was a short scare with rising damp that proved not to be a prob-lem. The veranda in the front had been an addition which I decided to keep but the old one had to go, it was rotten, and an ancient wisteria was pulling it down anyway. I found a painter who carefully, skilfully, slowly, painted the cornices and, a little faster, the walls. She did break a beautiful Solomon Island table when she fell off a ladder. Fortunately she was not injured.

As soon as it was habitable, I moved in, the finishing touches going on around me. My son came down to see what folly I had committed; he was impressed. I wanted a name for my house; he found a piece of old, discarded timber into which he carved my choice. He had asked if I was quite sure, to which I had replied in the affirmative.

New friends took me to the penny-farthing bicycle races, held an-nually at Evandale. On our wandering, I espied a bicycle leaning on a wall with a sign saying it was free to a good home. It was about eighty or ninety years old, in beautiful condition and its original gold lettering still readable. I asked my friends, if it was still there, unclaimed, by the time we were leaving, was there a way it could go on top of their car? So I was delivered home with a bicycle. I bought two cane baskets, one for the back, one for the front. The front one was filled with artificial flowers, the one at the back resembled a picnic, complete with a bottle of wine – well, the bottle at least, emptied, the cork replaced, and a book. It was positioned under the house name, 'WitzEnd'.

My desk was placed in the bay window of the drawing room. My street joined two busy roads, one each end, and had a private school, K to Grade 12, at the base of the hill on the corner. Pedestrian traffic could be busy as parents parked and walked their offspring to and from school each day. They couldn't miss the bicycle or the sign. It still gives me pleasure when I remember their smiles, and when they pointed them out to friends – not the finger-pointing indicators but conversation and the direction of eyes or a slight inclination on the head. And with my artisans, this gentility, the creative energy, the friendliness of the people, I knew I was home.

Prophecy

A dozen men and women sat in a rough circle in the open space of what was one of the meeting rooms of Australia's Parliament House. It was roofed, and sliding walls slid out from the curved wall that was part of the more secure building. In the past one and a quarter century, the weather had changed dramatically but the last fifty years had seen it settle into the pattern it would maintain for the next several hundreds. A scrap of historical reference, a white woman in the beginning of the twenty-first century believed in a future wet centre; the natural lake, unlike the man-made one in Canberra, was full, the Todd flowed and, like populations everywhere, the people had become used to the temperature extremes. Rail lines criss-crossed the country, fewer planes traversed the skies and those coming to Australia had to land at one of the coastal airports from where passengers took a super-fast train to their destination.

In this year of 2143, the country was celebrating seventy-five years of the Australian capital being Alice Springs. Elected politicians of all parties were roughly equal in terms of gender and colour; the token recognition towards Christianity had long since gone. The Lord's Prayer was no longer recited, all faiths were accepted and the country had never been so true to itself. Crime all but disappeared and conversation was meaningful. Australia enjoyed the distinction of having the longest habitation of one people and their culture of over sixty thousand years was as strong as ever.

Because of this ethnic mix, art, architecture, the built environment as well as the rural areas and, of course, menus, changed. It really did look as if the people had talked to each other and were not so pigheaded as to insist 'their' way was best. There was a unifying force bringing it all together; architects' designs took in such factors as needs of all sections of the community and the buildings had style. Apartments, two per floor, built above a commercial level with very few being more than nine storeys high, formed a circle, square, oval. There was space between each block and the centre ground became the recreational area. This way, children could be overlooked from the windows around and the workers were not isolated from general life for the active one-third of each day. A generally happier environment.

Peter Ambernoor's DNA would tell you his ancestors came from just about everywhere, with people following religions major and almost unheard of. Almost everyone on the planet could repeat this story and it was true; with each mixed marriage, the offspring inherited the best of each side. Different cultures continued to grow in the locations of their beginnings and individuals still enjoyed travel to explore these differences. Difference was celebrated. He looked at the members of the committee and the small gathering of interested people and thought of how much had happened in the more than seven decades, less than a lifetime for almost a hundred per cent of the planet's people. It's as if the room itself is smiling, he thought, himself happy but also aware of the great changes and the responsibilities that came with them.

Visitors from everywhere, including Australians from the various parts of what is still a very large country, will be here. Many are here already, enjoying the food, now truly Australian with less beef, lamb and pork, and what was available was imported quick-frozen. The pop-up shops included exhibitions of Australia's diverse arts and crafts. The main event, a non-stop drama going over three days and nights, will tell the Dreamtime stories, sixty thousand years old but still new to the modern world, kept hidden until the right time came. Guests will be able to come and go as they like; the artists will also come and go but in a worked-out rhythm. Invited guests, officials, will be staying in a variety of accommodations, each run by a different skin group, each keeping alive its original language, food preferences in line with the original totems, although in ordinary daily life these were not rules that had to be obeyed. Keeping alive a history does not have to be lived every day.

Pete, current chair of Parliament, with his office of workers, checked the speeches to be made, and made sure every detail was correct. Visitors would be landing at every airport and ongoing travel by rail had to be safe, not affected by sudden weather changes, one of the biggest bugbears in today's world.

There were checks again that the accommodations for the individual groups were not the same as the ones they stayed in last time they came. This was how visitors learned the diversity of Australia. Elders were not just Australian but included those who had managed to get away from the doomed villages and towns of the now frozen north and south bands of the planet. Pete knew this encouraged the elders to talk of past times; there were those who had been teenagers at the ceremony to announce Alice as the new capital and the young people learned history.

'I was here for that one,' wheezed an old man. 'Seventy-five years ago, more than your lifetime, Pete,' he said, eyes soft as he looked at the first speaker. 'I'd been living here four or five years by then, supposed to be moving on, but you know how it is – your mum was settled here already. That was the first visit of your gran, too, that festival. She loved it. Came every winter after that. If she came by plane, she'd start by describing the patterns below – the colours, textures, how she wished she could paint it. Gave her an aerial photo and she started buying local paintings. Course, can't see that any more but I'd rather have the limited air routes we have now. Now, we see as our ancestors did, by understanding light and shade, looking at shadows, reflections on rock, in water.

'She'd look at the range against the sky. It wasn't just the colours, orange-red against the blue, grey-green lower down – she felt something, then she'd have to go and find the nearest hill and actually touch it. Connecting, she said. Centenary of Federation, it was – 2001. Earlier ancestors were here for that, prob'ly the beginning of this story. She'd be so excited now, eh. Prob'ly try to run the show, though.' He stopped, breathing hard, the silence broken only by the odd chuckle from the three or four elders who remembered Peter's grandmother and told Fred he was getting his stories mixed.

They knew he'd start again and, although there was much to do, they liked hearing him talk. He was ninety-four, been around a long time, much loved and revered. And time was different here, in the Centre. 'The quality of the air, the deep spirituality, that mostly quiet passion that was in everything, the trees, rocks, waterholes, made the ticking of clocks meaningless. Time here was forever, old, now, then, nothing, everything. Space and matter are the same. And things were done, it was felt, as if seamlessly.'

One of the Arrernte elders thought of that Yeperenye Festival in 2001. The Elders, now, had the freshest stories. It was their immediate ancestors who were here then. His father had been one of the schoolkids, with his lantern, in the long procession. It had been a cold night, everyone said that, and there'd been delays, but his slight shiver now was more from the excitement he felt through his father's words, His pride and the passion he'd felt for his place, and how proud he would be now. All kids born in Alice Springs had been encouraged to participate, he remembered. Part of his tribe's inclusiveness. They didn't harbour hate or hold grudges; deep inside they felt pity for their gaolers, the pale men who didn't understand the land or its people. Yes, they'd shed many tears over the stolen children and the young men who died confined in small dark rooms. Our spirit needs the air, earth, sky. No, they didn't fight, not really, for their belief in their Dreaming never wavered and they knew, eventually, they would all find their own place.

The old man's thoughts were on the grand spectacle that told the story of the caterpillars, their journeys and struggles, their cocoons releasing the beautiful hawk moths, until their final metamorphosis into the McDonnell Range.

Corroborees happen, not regularly but often enough, when the Elders think one is needed. They don't tell the same stories but whichever part of history is pertinent to the moment. He thought of his own journeys, his struggles, the invisible hooks that prevented him from going too far away from the Centre once he'd arrived. On the surface, it seemed his kind of place. The weather, the laid-back lifestyle called to him. But his passions ran deep like those of this place. He thought of his own achievements and the progress of the town, the rapid changes, a certain transience of population but those who stayed, the good friends – all important. He felt close to the heart here, protected. He could understand the creativity that flowed from the centre. He chuckled at the thought of the big beanie exhibition, wearable art now developed into an international event.

'Hey,' he said aloud, 'where are the photos of that festival?'

'Which festival, Fred? You've been off on some trip of your own,' one of the women said.

'Yar, that Yeperenye in 2001. The Centenary of Federation.'

A young teenage girl, who had stopped close by to listen said, 'Hey, Uncle, they're all in the museum. Did you forget that? If you want to see them, I can set up a time for you. I'll take you if you want.'

'What about the poems?'

'Yep, all there, away from the light. Auntie May took you last month, remember?'

'Can you remember to say that welcome one?'

'Think so…' and her young, clear voice recited.

>Welcome to my land, brothers, sisters
>you, who have come across the sea
>and mountain range
>to this federation of many flags
>and languages
>Let us share our dance and song,
>brothers, sisters
>Welcome to the family of One…
>the lost, the stolen, come –
>join under sun, the moon, the stars
>that belong to no one –
>brothers, sisters
>but belong to all
>the whole world through.

Blackfella, whitefella, welcome
brothers, sisters.
Follow the Caterpillar tracks
to Yeperenye Dreaming
and if your spirit has been lost
revive it here
brothers, sisters.
Children, candle-bright
carry forward hope
while understanding history
and the passions of the mountain
range the beauty and the drama
that is here, brothers, sisters.

'It was that time those planes flew into the Twin Towers in New York,' said the old man after a pause. 'That was when the mob here started talking about faith and belief and one creator. A new corroboree was made about it.'

'Yes,' said another of the Arrernte elders, 'we were luckier here, keeping our space, more in touch with our life. But we never objected to the idea of a place where everybody could gather and pray to their own gods. That competition caused a bit of a fuss, all round the world. Some leaders said it would never work, others said why not and the folk who thought it up didn't know what an avalanche of entries they'd get. I reckon it showed there are more people with vision than not. One of the letters in the paper said it would look like an elephant as described by four blind men but there it is, just down the street apace, another of Australia's great buildings and used for the purpose of praying. Two of our newly graduated architects from here won it. Buildings around the world with their names on them, now. I think of a bird, yes, a bird, circling in the air then landing, shuffling to get comfy then ruffling its feathers and all the people of every faith falling out. Aye, I just see them, shaking each other's hands and saying how beautiful it is. Hey, isn't Birdie one of their kids or grandkids?'

The old man took up the story. 'I suppose it helped then that Jews and Moslems, Christians have different days of worship so they fit their times around each other. Hindus and Buddhists worked in with the others and there's the great centre for corroboree. It all flows, no corners, and you can see the sky – no roof over the middle and light pours in from all directions to the other sections. Comes back to being at the centre, the heartbeat of the country.'

Pete quietly tapped the table, but enough to get the attention of the group. 'Okay,' he said, 'can we get back to business here. The first visitors for this event will start arriving in three weeks and we need to check, double check, that everything will go smoothly. Twenty-five years on'll be the centenary, so this is like a dress rehearsal.'

The to and fro of conversation, the checking of lists, times of arrivals, respective accommodations, catering, being mindful of dietary laws, forms of address – some kings and queens, clergy, still favoured formality – it seemed endless but the youngsters, winners of citizen awards, sat quietly, taking it in and those elders, there mostly out of respect, nodded and made only the occasional remark. The old man's thoughts went back forty-six years, to the birth of his son, Rod, president-elect of the Republic of Australia.

Who would have thought it then, he mused to himself. We'd just got the train right through from Adelaide to Darwin. The beginning of the criss-crossing of lines across the country: more ecologically sensitive than roads. This Centre, the birth of so much. World peace started here, I reckon. As soon as that mob stopped all climbing on Uluru, there was an energy surge and things happened. Eh, the first time my mum saw it, it was raining. A group of Japanese tourists were there and she kept on telling them how lucky they were to see it in the rain. Bright sunshine next day and she thought she was blessed, seeing it wet and dry. She felt it was completely friendly, benevolent. Funny how I remember things from way back, don't know what I had for lunch yesterday. She was interested in rock, the different formations. He turned to tug at the young girl's arm, 'What was that rocky one?' he whispered.

Just as quietly the girl recited,

Those interior textures
flinty, glinty, sharp
as history.
Dry bright colours of mountain
clash with unbroken blue
of clear sky.
Laughter bouncing in the hills
the sound sometimes turns
to thunder.
And god's great lightning spark
gives birth to fire that cleans
and kills
making ready for new life.

He remembered the birth of his son, quiet, strong and whose name will go into the history books. Sort of prophetic, in a way, his string of names. Each one important to someone, his mother, me, his grandparents. The mixed blood, indicated by choice of names, contributed to his love of words and music, justice and leadership. Words, he thought. All the grandparents waiting for the birth, playing word games, the women trying not to remember the pain. For the naming ceremony, all their friends met up on Undoolya Hill. Late afternoon, his mother had described the weather as 'soft'; strange word to describe weather but it was a lovely warm winter afternoon. They watched the sun go down and a full moon rise. Words said, toasts made, food eaten. His mum, my darling wife, got most of the way through what she'd wanted to say and then got too emotional. Gave the bits of paper to me, but I didn't do it justice. Pretty quickly asked mum to say a few words. Bit of a worry there 'cause you never knew if she was going to be able to stop. She didn't go over the top, though. He let out a sigh and then remembered with a grin the clean-up before they left. They turned on the headlights – everyone drove their own cars then. How wasteful. Now, no one drives and cars are borrowed – but yes, then, everyone collected wine corks, wrappers, everything they'd brought in. Second nature to them all.

She wrote about the naming, too – did she know?

We were high,
up on Undoolya Hill;
wrapped, in something soft
like air, the breeze, on a tissue of light.
God's gentle gleaming eye, soft breath aloft.
we knew the babe belonged to us
yet naming gave no lock and key;
passing over Alice town
the wind breathed, he is free.
The friends who gathered there
brought love, soft toys and sparkling wine
adding to the Centre's shine.
And yes, there's rubbish in the river bed
an old man sleeping in the street
but they didn't ask for us to come
and time it takes for minds to meet.
Minds to sort out differences
find the point of mutual good
and turn the key
to stop the flood
of mild indifference
or cruel…bitter…hate.
But first to find the lock
and the words that say 'I'm sorry',
not just for him
but those who used a different, older, clock.
Destiny, that day, would not be ignored –
it gave the gift of leadership which can be
blessing and a curse
but scarce were those who would oppose,
the few won by the many.
The babe spoke early,
from the heart, taught his peers to share
then led debates and healed the weary
everything within him true.

The talk continued around him and the days turned into weeks until the day arrived. Excitement was electric, sparking. He watched as dignitaries were shown to their seats. The huge marquee filled, the loud-speakers and TV screens outside had been checked. Not only here, but people all around the world would be watching this.

His son walked to centre stage and started to speak. 'Thank you, thank you…' He paused, his words hardly heard above the cheering and shouting and clapping of the crowd. His face was one big smile as he raised his hands, waving in a downward motion, asking for silence and for the audience to regain their seats as he said again, 'Thank you. It gives me great pleasure to welcome all of you. For those who have travelled a great distance, welcome to the heart of this great nation and into our own individual hearts. At the special corroboree this morning, the Arrernte people welcomed and blessed you. I honour and give thanks to the ancient custodians of land, spirit, Dreaming through their descendants.'

Both his hands went to rest on the lectern, his head bent and in the several seconds of silence, thoughts whirling, the enormity of his task threatening to overcome him, he drew on the strength, the passion, that is the Centre. He pictured those places, a rock, a tree, that were 'his', places of comfort and inspiration. The people important in his life, parents, friends, children, elders – some gone to their own Dreaming but still with him, giving him strength, slid through his mind.

His body relaxed and he looked up, continuing, 'Today, midway through the twenty-second century, we are gathered to celebrate the new status of this nation. That did take some time to achieve but what did not was the changing of the capital of Australia from Canberra to Alice Springs. When the idea was first put forward, it gathered momentum and quickly arrived at the conclusion. Not everyone agreed with a republican Australia but the strength and passion that is and flows from, the Centre could not be denied and both these things are now reality.

'One of my friends,' here his eyes rested on the tall black man in the front row, 'gathered his strength and that of his spirit ancestors to become head of the United Nations. And the emphasis is on 'united', for now the world is. We are all free to be, to roam, to return. We all know where 'home' is and we are free to go there. There is a saying, 'Home is where the heart is,' and the heart of this country is here. We came to know it; the people of Country have always known it.

'In 2001, this country celebrated the Centenary of Federation. The first event was New Dawn, held on the red desert plains not far from here. In the September, it was the great Yeperenye Festival. Indigenous people from all parts of Australia travelled here and told their stories through dance and song. Paintings, artefacts, were on display. The Arrernte people showed their generosity and inclusiveness by insisting that all Alice Springs-born children be invited to participate in the enactment of the Caterpillar Dreaming. The simple caterpillars, going through their life stages, not without struggle as ours fought with the Stinky Beetle Men but eventually becoming the ranges now forming part of the horizon before you. As history, on a large scale, and our lives on a smaller one, go through various rites of passage. Our particular journey has brought us to this point in history. National history and a point in individual lives that will be talked of by our descendants.

'The impact of that spectacle was not just visual. It awakened in people, both Australian citizens and visitors, a hunger to know more of the history of this land. For the history stretches back many thousands of years before the planting of the British flag. I believe the country started to come of age when people wanted to know the ancient past and become part of today's culture that will one day itself become ancient.

'We lost some of our arrogance and realised the importance of indigenous languages. Unfortunately, some were already lost, but with both hands the others were tightly grasped. More teachers were trained so they could teach in their own languages with English as a second subject. This expanded to teaching Aboriginal cultures. Many of you here today have entrusted your children to the care of one or other of our excellent boarding schools. In including Indigenous studies, we realised we were losing touch with Western classics and philosophy. We saw the sense of a fully rounded education and today our graduating students can go anywhere, do anything.

'I have been saying "we" but I had no part in it. I was not born until after the Yeperenye Festival and grew up with the evolving ideas of my elders. I became interested in republicanism and it felt right that government should flow from the centre. When I was born, the competition for a design for an all-faiths building was in full swing. I was well into my teens before the building was completed. You can imagine it caused controversy. Sometimes it seemed it would be the cause of World War III but quiet dignity, strength of belief, gently held it together and after many consultations with all concerned, we have the first building of its kind. Its separate parts flow into the whole. This morning you sat in the centre, open to the sky, for your welcoming corroboree. Other events will be held there as well as in the other sacred areas, in the coming days.

'You will see the creativity that stretches in a multitude of directions covering art and science. Traditional work is on display, with young artists keeping the essence of tradition but some new innovation creeping in. There are multidimensional ecological displays. It is an understatement to say that we are proud.

'It is my belief that passion begets passion and as we all observe, respect, the passions of the ancient Dreaming, that passion comes into us, allowing for the creativity, the peace, that flows from the Centre. Before you all, I again humbly seek the blessings of the Ancients as well as the working hands and minds close by as I assume the role of President of the Republic of Australia. Thank you.'

And the cheers reached the outermost stars.